A Memory So Sweet

Sunrise Sisters Trilogy

OLIVIA MILES

ROSEWOOD PRESS

979-8986262444 (print)
A Memory So Sweet

This is a work of fiction. Names, characters, places, and incidents are a product of the author's imagination. Locales and public names are sometimes used for atmospheric purposes. Any resemblance to actual people, living or dead, or to businesses, companies, events, institutions, or locales is completely coincidental.

also by olivia miles

Blue Harbor Series

A Place for Us

Second Chance Summer

Because of You

Small Town Christmas

Return to Me

Then Comes Love

Finding Christmas

A New Beginning

Summer of Us

A Chance on Me

Evening Island

Meet Me at Sunset

Summer's End

The Lake House

Oyster Bay Series

Feels Like Home

Along Came You

Maybe This Time

This Thing Called Love

Those Summer Nights

Christmas at the Cottage

Still the One

One Fine Day

Had to Be You

Misty Point

One Week to the Wedding

The Winter Wedding Plan

Briar Creek Series

Mistletoe on Main Street

A Match Made on Main Street

Hope Springs on Main Street

Love Blooms on Main Street

Christmas Comes to Main Street

Harlequin Special Edition

'Twas the Week Before Christmas

Recipe for Romance

ONE

The way Carly Parker saw it, there were two sorts of people in life: the ones who held out hope and the ones who'd long ago given up on it.

Carly fell into the first category, earning her various nicknames in her childhood that she'd rather forget (Sunny, Sunshine, Little Ray, to state the obvious). There was the school talent show that she signed up for every year even though she couldn't dance, sing, or even do a cartwheel. (Okay, she couldn't do a somersault either, despite her older sisters' efforts.) Still, people clapped, as people in a small town with a population of under one thousand are wise to do, because you never knew who you might run into in the produce section or at the post office the next day.

Bouts of optimism prevailed in other forms too: the library's thrice annual coloring contest, which she never once won. Never. Once. There was the garden she'd planted each spring with her grandmother's help: one with vegetables that she planned to eat and flowers that she intended to clip. By July, the rabbits had eaten the tulip heads and the always surprisingly small tomatoes that never did have a chance to turn red. The hydrangeas always failed to bloom, and she seemed to forget each winter that worms made her scream. By August, she was deflated, sure, but by March, she was looking forward again. Telling herself that this time it would be different. This time she'd have a harvest—wicker baskets overflowing with tomatoes as big as her hands and oh, maybe an herb garden to go with them. And vases full of roses, which never did seem to like her in the past, but this time it would be different.

She told herself that again now, as she gripped the steering wheel, slowing only slightly as the sign to Hope Hollow approached.

This time would be different.

This time, things would work out.

After all, she wasn't ten anymore, losing the only parent she ever knew. Or a broken-hearted teenager, relying on the years ahead to give her a fresh start. She was a cool, twenty-eight-year-old woman of the world, one with experiences under her belt. One with perspective. One who knew that all the love and best of intentions didn't guarantee a happy ending. But still...there was hope.

And a chance—to finally earn a regular column at the lifestyle magazine where she'd worked since graduating from college in Philadelphia. For years she'd proofread other columnists' work, sometimes being granted a feature piece, but never on a regular basis. And now it was within reach; even if it did require a trip back to her hometown.

Main Street seemed quiet for a Thursday afternoon, but then, maybe that was unfair of Carly. It couldn't compete with city traffic, which had been a little unsettling at first but now felt comfortable, reassuring even. If so many people could decide to be in one spot at any given moment of any day of the week, then surely she'd made the right decision in joining them?

Surely. Absolutely. Or so she kept telling herself.

Carly's eyes roved over the storefronts of the quiet Connecticut town, which hadn't changed much with time: coffeehouse, pizza parlor, a few pubs, the ice cream shop, bookstore, hardware shop (that was, ironically, still missing two of the letters in its sign), clothing shops, home boutiques, and of course, the bakery.

Most people would probably call Sunrise Bakery the best place in all of Hope Hollow and Carly would be one of them. Generations of Parkers had treated their neighbors to sweets, been a central part of every celebration, and helped the local dentist build a thriving practice. Nana Parker had trained Carly and her sisters from a young age, instructing them on everything from crimping a perfect crust to whipping cream into soft peaks.

Carly's stomach tightened with anticipation as she pulled into the closest parking spot to the bakery that she could find, which was only three storefronts down and across the street, and grabbed her handbag from the passenger seat, where it had kept her company for the last four hours.

Yes, some people had spouses to fill the spot next to them. Others, children. Some, a pet. She had a handbag that had cost five months of savings and a promise to herself to make it last a full ten years. A proper, adult handbag. An investment. Dimes on the day, if you did the math. Really, you could justify anything with a little creativity.

Which was exactly how Carly justified being here, in her sleepy hometown, standing at the corner of Oak and Main and wondering if anyone would notice her before she had a chance to greet her family. Word would spread—that was the problem. Say, if Debbie over at the flower shop happened to come outside right now to water her enviably healthy petunias. (Dreams of that garden bloomed once more, even though it would have to be of the container variety, seeing as Carly's only source to the outside world these days was a balcony off her one-bedroom apartment. Okay, it was a fire escape.) Debbie would greet Carly with warmth and a hundred questions, the answers to which she would then rush inside to tell Maria at the pizza parlor over a barely whispered phone call, with both women's noses pressed against the glass windows of their storefronts that faced Main Street, watching as Carly crossed. By the time Carly hit the other side of the street, Maria would be scurrying outside as fast as her round form would allow her, asking Carly to come in for her famous tiramisu, and Carly would be forced to explain that she couldn't today, that she was on her way to the bakery.

And there, at Sunrise Bakery, the phone in the bustling kitchen would ring until one of her sisters or her grandmother dusted the flour off her hands and answered, and Maria (or Debbie, who really wanted to be the one to break this news) would announce Carly's arrival just as she was pushing through the door.

Carly could only hope that the oversize sunglasses she'd treated herself to for Christmas last year would do the trick. There were the new honey highlights in her hair, too. And of course, the fact that she hadn't stepped foot in Hope Hollow in a solid ten years.

No one would notice her because no one expected her to ever return to this little town that was so full of memories. Not even her family.

Sunrise Bakery looked exactly the same as it did the last time Carly had been here, which was not much different than it had looked when Carly started working here with her sisters, around the time she was old enough to pour chocolate chips into batter and punch out Christmas cookies with the cutters that had been passed down from her maternal great-grandparents.

Outside, the yellow awning bore the store's logo, and the glass-paned door was centered between two large windows, one featuring some sweets to entice passersby, the other giving a view of a few of the patrons sitting at tables.

Carly felt a wave of nostalgia at the sight of the old place, but the nerves that tightened her stomach when she reached for the brass handle of the front door nearly made her run back to the car to collect herself. She hadn't told anyone she was coming. It was last minute, and, if she was being honest with herself, she wasn't exactly sure she'd be completely welcome.

She nearly chickened out when a teenage boy appeared behind her and shuffled his feet impatiently.

"Are you going in?"

She took a deep breath and nodded. Yep. She was going in.

Inside, the walnut floorboards were scuffed and faded from the sun that poured through the south-facing floor-to-ceiling windows each afternoon. The display case that ran the length of the room was filled with homemade cookies, brownies, muffins, tarts, and cakes. On the back counter, the stainless-steel cappuccino machine hissed while Becca, Carly's middle sister, worked hard at foaming the milk, which Carly knew she'd pour into a pretty design in the mugs that had been printed with the shop's logo. Her yellow-and-white-striped apron had a few chocolate smudges near the waist, and as Carly hung back, waiting for her sister to hand over the drink, she noticed that Becca's dark brown hair was coming loose from its messy bun.

In other words, very little had changed in Carly's absence and she was grateful for that. Sure, she hadn't been home in longer than she cared to admit, but there was still something about being able to come home, knowing that it would always be the way she'd left it, that filled her soul nearly as much as the smell of those macaroons that her oldest sister Jill was now carrying out on a tray.

The tray went down with a thud—on the counter, luckily, though Carly knew that Jill could whip up another batch in a few minutes if need be.

"Carly!"

Now it was Becca who quickly set down the hot mug, fortunately not spilling a drop (but then she was no stranger to surprises, that one), and started coming around the counter.

It felt like a hundred questions all at once as her sisters both pulled her in for a hug, immune to the stares from the patrons who sat at the wood tables, clustered cozily together, their chairs mismatched but each one comfortable.

"Does Nana know you're coming?" Jilly finally asked.

"No, but with all this raucous I'm surprised she hasn't come out by now." Carly glanced over Becca's shoulder toward the kitchen. "I'll go back and say hi."

"Oh." Her sisters exchanged a glance before Becca explained, "She...isn't here today."

"Not here today?" Carly couldn't fight back her disappointment. She'd spoken to her grandmother just last week and she'd given no indication of any time off or a trip. "Well, I guess I'll see her later at the house." Now she wondered if she should have announced this visit yesterday when her editor sent her off on this assignment—the one she couldn't wait to tell her sisters and grandmother about, once she had them all together.

Now, she realized that wouldn't be today.

But, there was always tomorrow, the optimist in her said!

"So you're staying at the house? How long are you here for?" Jill looked more curious than pleased, which, given the unexpected nature of the visit, was probably fair.

"That's undecided," Carly said vaguely, feeling the first hint of anxiety overshadow her good mood. Ever since she'd pitched the idea of highlighting the success of a multi-generational, family-owned small business to her editor, she'd alternated between kicking herself and imagining a new desk, in a proper office, not the windowless cube she'd spent her days in for too many years to admit. She had two weeks to write her story and present it along with two other coworkers vying for the same position. But a story like this would practically write itself. She'd grown up in these walls and watched familiar faces enter at their usual times for their usual orders. Memorized Nana's recipes which never changed and never would.

"Oh, the line is backing up!" Becca looked flustered as she stepped away, but Carly just waved off her concerns.

"I should go to the house anyway and see Nana."

"No!" Jill's blue eyes were bright as she smiled. "I mean, we're closing up soon. Sit, stay. We can catch up over coffee. You can see Nana later."

Carly shrugged. "Okay." And a warm drink did sound good after such a long drive. "But only if I can have a slice of that streusel cake."

"Sold out." Jill looked proud at that statement. "But I can get you a slice of chocolate silk pie."

Now Carly felt the weight of her problems roll off her shoulders. There was little better in this world than her family's chocolate silk pie. Even she didn't know the secret ingredient. Yet.

She found a table near the window with a view of Main Street and admired the window boxes that were filled with pansies in all different colors. A quick look around the room proved that she didn't know any of the customers at the moment, but that could all change, even in the next thirty minutes or so before closing.

"Here you go." Jill was perky when she delivered the coffee and pie—an extra-large slice and not just because they were nearing closing time.

Carly smiled in gratitude and realized with a lump in her throat just how much she had missed her oldest sister, even though she'd seen her last winter when she'd visited Philly.

Correction: that had been two winters ago. Becca visited with her grandmother since then but Jill stayed behind, using the bakery as an excuse.

"I'm glad you're back. Surprised, but glad." Jill tipped her head, showing none of the resentment that sometimes strained their relationship over the years since Carly had left town. "At some point, I'm going to ask what made you come," she warned before walking off.

Carly nodded. She was ready, having prepared her pitch for most of the drive, but now she wavered. Her sisters hadn't been supportive of her decision to leave town, not when they'd all been groomed from an early age to take over the bakery. Had time washed away the hard feelings? She'd find out soon enough, she supposed, just like she'd soon know whether she was getting a promotion or be stuck at a dead-end job. She wasn't the most talented of the group going for the position.

But she was the one putting her heart into it, even though she'd tried to close that off a long time ago.

Carly slid her spoon through the creamy chocolate-filled

pie and took a moment to enjoy the feeling of it resting on her tongue and melting in her mouth.

There was very little that chocolate silk pie couldn't fix in this world, or so she'd always believed.

Now, she was counting on it.

When the last customer begrudgingly left for the day, the door was locked behind them and the sign turned, Jill and Becca joined Carly at the table. Both of them were still wearing their aprons and Carly knew that there would be plenty of work to do in the kitchen before they went home for the night.

She considered offering to help until she remembered that she still hadn't told her grandmother she was in town— or needed a place to stay.

"There's something you should know," Jill said. "About Nana."

Something cold ran through Carly's chest. She told herself to calm down, that it couldn't be that bad because if it was then surely she would have heard something, if not from her sisters than from her friend Joanna, whom she spoke with regularly.

Still, she wasn't successful in stopping the panic that caused her heart to speed up. She asked tightly, "What about Nana?"

She had lost track of her grandmother's age (not that Nana was open to such discussion). She'd always been so sprite, ever since Carly could remember, even when she'd taken them all into her house—her daughter and three granddaughters. Nana had been widowed by then already, happy for the company, keeping busy running the bakery with the help of her only daughter right up until the fateful diagnosis.

Now Carly thought about that time, even though she tried not to. Coming back was already stirring up those memories that were so much easier to tuck away out in Philly.

"Is she...sick?" she managed.

"No!" Becca quickly assured her. "Nothing like that."

Carly's shoulders dropped with relief. "I didn't think so. I just talked to her on the phone last week and everything was fine." That did little reassure her, though, as did the glance her sisters exchanged across the table.

It was nothing new—this connection her sisters shared that she lacked. They were older, closer in age, and they had a special bond with the bakery that she hadn't shared, maybe because she'd always felt a little bit like an outsider, even though they were all three known as the "Sunrise Sisters" around town, or, when their grandmother was having a particularly long day in their adolescent years, "the three tarts."

Now, Carly saw that Jill and Becca had only grown closer with time and, more likely, proximity.

"Nana doesn't work at the bakery anymore," Becca explained.

"She *retired*?" Carly blinked, taking in this information. Their grandmother practically lived at the bakery. She always said it was her home away from home, that walking in the door each morning and serving her customers was as good for her heart as it was theirs.

And though she never said it, all three of the Parker sisters knew that mixing a batter or frosting a cake or kneading out a loaf of her famous rosemary bread was the only thing that got Nana through the loss of her husband and later, her daughter, when Carly was only ten years old.

"Her arthritis has been getting worse. She hasn't made her bread in months, and she probably should have stopped before that." Jill pushed her ponytail off her shoulder. Of all of them, she looked the most like their mother with her bright blue eyes and nut-brown hair.

But when it came to personality, she was all Nana.

"But—what will she do without the bakery?" The real question was, who would she be? Before her sisters had a chance to answer, Carly said, "Why didn't she tell me?"

"She probably didn't see a reason to upset you." Becca shrugged.

"Why didn't either of you tell me?" Carly's voice rose even as she recognized her own part in things. Her calls with her sisters weren't exactly frequent, and now she realized with shame that she hadn't spoken to either of them since the holidays.

Still. This was big news. And the phone worked both ways.

Jill sighed. "Honestly, I didn't think you were that interested in the bakery."

Carly stared at her sister. She opened her mouth and then closed it again. There was plenty she could say to set Jill straight, but that would be a long conversation and there was a bigger issue at hand.

"I'm very interested in Nana's health." The emotion in her voice wasn't lost on Jill, who glanced down at her hands. As the table fell silent, Carly knew that she wasn't the only one thinking of their mother, of how scary it had been when she first got sick, and how difficult it had been to lose her.

"Nana is fine for the most part. But she's getting on in age and it was becoming too much for her," Jill explained in a softer tone.

"In many ways, it was a long time coming. Nothing stays the same forever." Becca gave her a sad smile and Carly nodded. It was true, and they of all people knew that best.

"That's not all…" Now Jill didn't meet her eyes and Becca had started to brush at the stains on her apron, as if she could actually scrape them off. "Without Nana's help, it's just been the two of us, and business hasn't really been the same lately, since so many people came in just to see Nana. Our overhead has gone up steadily each year, and the price of ingredients, too. But there's only so much we can charge for a slice of pie."

"What are you saying?" Carly asked with growing dread.

Jill looked at her flatly. "We've had an offer on the bakery."

"An *offer*? What does that even mean?" Carly blinked rapidly, trying to keep up with developments she couldn't have even imagined.

"It means that someone's offered to come in and take over. Free us up, make our lives easier." Jill looked defensive now as she leaned back in her chair. It creaked from age. "We need new ovens, something's always breaking, and Becca and I have to entertain this offer. We have to think about our futures."

"But what about the future of the bakery? This is our family's bakery," Carly reminded her sisters, leaning across the table. "Nana won't share the recipes with anyone else."

"Oh, we know," Jill snorted. "And that's part of the problem. She won't let us hire any new staff. Family only is the policy."

Always was.

"Nothing's official...yet," Becca assured her, but the pause in her wording didn't give Carly much reason to hope.

"Does Nana know?"

Becca nodded. "Things have changed. She knows first-hand how much work it is to keep this place going."

"Well, this certainly wasn't what I was expecting," Carly said with a huff. She realized now just how foolish she'd been, a mere moment ago, thinking that everything was exactly as she'd left it, like it had been waiting for her.

"You haven't told us what brought about this visit." Becca's tone brightened but her smile didn't quite meet her eyes.

"Oh..." Carly struggled for an excuse, knowing that now wasn't the time to get into the details of her return. With a sinking feeling, she considered the fact that the reason may now be moot. A featured story on a small-town bakery that was about to be sold to the highest bidder wasn't exactly what she had pitched to her editor.

"I just thought it was about time," she finally said. Only she might just be too late.

Becca gave a tired sigh. "Well, we'd better get back to work or we'll be here all night. And we still have to box up the leftovers."

Every evening, it was tradition for their family to box up what hadn't sold and donate it to the community. Sometimes it was the soup kitchen in the neighboring town, or a snack for the hospital staff three towns over, other times they distributed it to some of the older people in town, or people just needing to be reminded that they were thought of during a hard time.

"I can do the run on my way to the house," Carly offered. She wasn't in the same rush to get there, not with this news, and not while she was still processing it. Her grandmother no longer worked at Sunrise Bakery. It didn't seem possible.

"Thanks." Jill stretched her back and stifled a yawn. "I think it's going over to the recreation center today."

Becca was already checking the calendar on her phone. "Nope. It's the fire station today."

Carly was already gathering her tote. "Perfect. That's right on the way."

Becca's eyes flashed. "Maybe we should talk first."

But by now Carly had heard about enough. "Please don't," she said wearily. "I just got back and I've had about enough bad news for one day."

Becca opened her mouth and then closed it, her hazel eyes softening at the corners. "I'm just...happy you're back."

Carly nodded and then went to the counter to start boxing up what hadn't sold. She wished that she could say the same, but right now even she struggled to see the bright side.

Dusk was settling in when she walked back to her car, carrying the two paper bags loaded with items that hadn't sold. Was there always so much? She frowned, thinking of the days when they would have to close up early, sold out for the day. Nana never wanted to leave her neighbors and customers wanting more, but she was careful with inventory and had learned over time how much to bake each day.

As Carly set the bags in the front seat, moving her over-priced handbag to the floor, she thought of what that money for the bag could have done for the shop. Paid for those new ovens, perhaps. Kept things going another month or two.

Just looking at the bag was a reminder of her life in Philadelphia. The article she had to write. The promotion that was riding on it.

Even chocolate silk pie couldn't cure this problem.

With a sigh, she closed the passenger door and walked around to the driver's side, only breathing a little easier when she was tucked inside, back in her own world. The drive to the firehouse was short. In true small-town charm, the wood-sided building had been painted red, and a stone path led from the street where she parked to the glass-paned front door.

Carly set her bags down and reached for the handle just as something stopped her.

There, through the window, was a group of firefighters, some passing around a beanbag, others gathered around a table, eating pasta, no doubt cooked up by Frankie, Maria's son, who had been a volunteer firefighter for as long as Carly could remember, working in the kitchen of the pizza parlor the rest of the time.

And there, across the room, staring right at her, was Nick Sutton.

The one face she'd never expected to see in town.

Even if he was part of the reason she'd stayed away.

two

Nick Sutton considered himself jaded enough at this point in life that nothing could phase him anymore. But there was no denying the skip in his pulse when he saw the woman standing at the entrance of the fire station, holding two bakery bags, the pleasant smile on her face slipping the moment their eyes locked.

The beanbag that they passed around on downtime hit him square in the nose, pulling his attention from Carly. Across the room, some of the other guys laughed, and he probably would have too, a long time ago. But there was nothing funny about sitting here, staring at the only girl he'd ever hurt. Badly. And knowing that if he had to do it all over again, he wouldn't change a thing. That was the tough part about life. You didn't always get a choice, and when you did, it didn't always come easily, and certainly not without some casualties.

"Hey, is that Carly Parker? Or am I seeing a ghost?" Zach —one of his oldest friends who, like most people in this small town, knew the entire history of Nick's sordid love life —flashed him a look across the room before taking long strides across the room, his grin broad, his arms wide as he greeted Carly with a hug.

Jealousy panged even though if there was any Sunrise Sister that Zach would be interested in, it would be Jill. Nick closed his eyes briefly, remembering the feel of Carly in his arms, how her hair always smelled as sweet as the pies she baked, how her eyes would shine when they finally pulled apart.

He swallowed hard and stood up. To not cross the room and greet her wouldn't be right, but then everything that happened between him and Carly had felt so wrong in the end. There was no real way of making it easy, no going back, no undoing the past. He could only keep moving forward. At least that's what he'd been telling himself for the past ten years.

Her smile slipped slightly as Zach stepped to the side, relieving Carly of the bakery bags in the process. Her eyes which were once filled with light now seemed to be shadowed, mirroring the anxiety that churned in his stomach and drummed in his chest.

Behind him, the room seemed to grow quiet. Zach was walking away.

"Carly." Nick's voice was husky and he cleared his throat. He didn't even know what to say to her. There was so much he wanted to say but couldn't.

She gave a small smile, but it was a sad one. "Hello, Nick. This...I didn't...I didn't know you worked here."

So her family didn't mention him. He shouldn't be

stung. Why should they bring him up? For all he knew, Carly was married or engaged or had a serious boyfriend. But all he knew about her was that she worked for a magazine, based in Philadelphia, where she'd gone to college. He'd stopped himself from ever inquiring further, telling himself it didn't matter, that they'd had their chance. Life had pushed them together and then pulled them apart.

"I moved back from Boston about three years ago. How long has it been since you've been here?" He meant to lighten the mood, but her hazel gaze darkened.

"My family has been good about visiting me in Philly. I think my being there gives them an excuse to take a break a little more often."

He nodded. He knew that too. The trips to see her, sometimes closing the bakery for a long weekend. He always stopped short of telling one of her sisters or her grandmother to say hello to Carly for him. That felt selfish, somehow, all things considered.

"Is there...an emergency or something?" Her eyes grew round as she pointed to something in the distance behind him.

Nick turned around, stifling a grown when he saw everyone filing out of the room. Only Frankie remained at the table, forking a meatball and then twirling his spaghetti without shame or care.

Nick looked back at Carly and gave a small grin. "Looks like we cleared the place out. Well, except for Frankie. But it takes four alarms to pull him from the dinner table."

That brought a hint of the smile he'd always loved from her. One that nearly reached her eyes but not quite.

"So. A firefighter." She raised her eyebrows, surprised, no doubt.

It was unexpected, sure. Certainly not what he'd planned.

But as they both knew, plans could change. And they had.

"When I moved back here, I joined. Can't think of a better way to serve the community."

She nodded. The silence between them spoke a hundred words. Questions he wanted to ask. Things he wanted to say. He wondered if she'd ask about his child. He wondered if she knew whether he had a son or a daughter. Or if she'd ask about Liz. He hoped that she didn't because that had become something even he didn't understand.

"Are you in town for the weekend?" he asked before things went down a path he'd rather not go.

"A bit longer, actually. At least, that was the plan. Now, I'm not sure." Carly frowned a little, and he suspected that it had nothing to do with finding herself standing here, talking to him.

"Back to stay?" His heart reacted stronger than it had when he'd looked over and seen her standing at the door.

She laughed. Oh, the sound. He'd forgotten it over time —told himself that he had to. Now, he couldn't help but smile at the memory of her sitting beside him at the lake, the wind blowing her hair at her shoulders, her smile wide and that laugh filling his chest in a way he'd never known until then.

"No," she said firmly. "No, definitely no chance of that."

He wondered what she meant by that. If she was referring to him now living in Hope Hollow, or the rumor going around town that Sunrise Bakery might be closing down, or that she had an entire life—a good life—far from here.

Surely, it had nothing to do with him.

"That's a shame," he said before he caught himself. Her eyes flashed on his and he quickly added, "I mean, your sisters and grandmother must be happy to have you back."

She nodded. "I'm actually on my way to see my grandmother now. I just got in and she doesn't know I'm here, so…"

So it was time for her to go. End this awkward encounter. Get back to his shift.

He was almost hoping that alarm bell would sound—nothing major, not that there ever really was in this sleepy little town, but enough to give him an excuse to walk away.

Not look back.

Because that's what he'd done all those years ago. One foot in front of the other. He'd had no choice, not the way he saw it.

"I'll let you go."

She pulled in a breath and then gave a quick nod. She turned, reaching for the door handle, and the realization that this had happened, that after all these years he'd seen her again, hit him full force.

He wanted to explain, but what explanation was there? He wanted to apologize, but how could he if he'd make the choice all over again?

He wanted—he didn't know what he wanted. He just wanted to hold on to this feeling, hold onto her for a little bit longer.

"Carly."

She turned, looking at him expectantly. He could say anything. Something that would take back the past ten years, the hurt from the way they'd left things. He could say that he missed her, that he wished nothing but the best for her. That he was sorry.

He'd waited ten long years for this chance and here it was. And he didn't feel like it was his place to say anything. Ten years was a long time. He'd lived it well. Filled it as best he could.

And Carly, no doubt, had done the same.

"It was...good seeing you," he said.

She held his gaze for a moment, and for the second time in their lives, it seemed a shared understanding passed through the silence.

"Good night, Nick," she finally said, and then turned away.

He didn't know what he'd been expecting her to say, but he knew what he'd been hoping. And that wasn't it.

But then, he didn't really have any right to hold out hope when it came to Carly Parker, did he? She'd moved on with her life, and he was still waiting to see how his turned out.

Carly walked as quickly as her legs would allow her to the car with a pounding heart. She got inside, forcing herself to not look back, to peel out of that parking spot as quickly as the pavement would allow her to. She cranked up the music on the radio, but it did nothing to drown out the memories that played in her head on repeat.

That was something she and Nick used to do, that one, magical summer that felt like it would last forever. Climb into his old Jeep, roll down the windows, and crank up the volume. The wind would blow in their faces the entire drive out to Lake Hollow, and they'd sing the words to every song they knew—and some they didn't. She'd felt so free then, like anything was possible.

She shook her head now. Flicked off the radio. Tried to keep her focus on the road and off the pain that squeezed tight in her heart. Nana's house wasn't far from the center of town, nearly walkable, and for all the years that Carly had lived there, her grandmother had indeed often walked to the bakery most mornings, claiming that the cool air invigorated her and gave her the energy she needed to get through the long day.

Now, Carly realized with a sinking heart that Nana wouldn't be taking that early morning walk again. That she'd hung up her apron.

Just like Carly had all those years ago when leaving was easier than staying. When Hope Hollow seemed to remind her of every loss she'd ever known and no hope of a brighter future.

She turned down the next street, slowing as the old house appeared, looking from the outside as cherished as the bakery had once been. Now, Carly was worried about what she would discover inside. Would the house be different too? Was loss in this town just inevitable?

Nana Parker's house was her home long before her

mother died. When their father had packed his bags one morning and left them for what Carly later learned was another woman, her mother had decided that she was also in need of some change. And assistance. And maybe, a little adult company. She'd packed up the small house, listed it for sale, and moved them into the large wood-sided house where she'd grown up. When their own small house had finally sold, Carly's mother sank the profits directly into the bakery, where she'd worked right up until her health didn't let her anymore.

Carly had been ten when she lost her mother, but for years following, she still couldn't take a bite of a chocolate chip cookie without tasting the hint of cinnamon that her mother always added.

Without thinking of her. Her mother was a Parker, a fighter, strong and resilient like Nana, and the three sisters were determined to honor that legacy. When they were old enough, they each legally changed their last names from Parker-Fine to just Parker, united in their family history and the strong women who had come before them.

Carly pulled to a stop in the driveway. The navy-blue front door opened to the cedar-shingled house before Carly could even pop the trunk, and there, on the front steps, stood Nana Parker. Her grey hair was pulled back in her usual loose bun, and even in the dim lighting, Carly could see the spark in her blue eyes as she approached.

"I can't believe it's really true!" Nana sang out, opening her arms as she hurried down the front path at a brisk pace, even if she was wearing her fuzzy house slippers.

So much for a surprise, but then, there wasn't much

room for that when it came to the Parkers. They told each other everything—or had, once. They were a team, the five women, until they were down to four. Now, Carly supposed that with her absence they were reduced to three, and only two remained at the bakery.

Carly pushed all those worrying thoughts from her head as she pulled her grandmother in for a hug, breathing in her sweet smell—proof that she had been up to some baking, after all.

"Who told you?" she asked when they pulled back. "Jill?"

Jill was dutiful and diligent. She'd probably want to make sure that Nana was prepared for a guest, even though Nana always prided herself on keeping a clean house. She had to, she liked to say, considering how people in Hope Hollow popped over all the time.

But Carly hadn't popped over in years.

"No, it was actually Melissa down at the ice cream shop. She heard it from Pam, who heard it from Maria, of course."

Carly could only shake her head. Of course. It wouldn't have been any other way.

"I said I wouldn't believe it until I saw you for myself," her grandmother continued as they wandered back toward the front porch arm in arm. "Of course, that didn't stop me from making your favorite dessert. And I have some soup warming on the stove, too."

"Strawberry pie?" Carly didn't know whether to smile or cry. She dropped her handbag to the floor when they stepped inside the front hall, deciding to go back for her luggage later. Right now, she wanted to take in this feeling, of being here, in the old house she'd shared with her sisters, and once, her mother. But first, she gave a disapproving look toward her grandmother. "But Nana. Your arthritis."

Her grandmother's face flushed. "So they told you then. What else did they say?"

Pretty much everything other than the fact that Nick Sutton was back in town.

"They told me that you're considering closing the bakery," Carly replied.

Her grandmother huffed out a breath. "Come on back to the kitchen. I'll put on some coffee."

Carly took her time walking down the hallway, past the living room where silver frames lined the mantle, her grandfather's favorite leather chair, scratched and faded though it now was, still holding court in the corner under the brass reading lamp. Carly's chest ached as she looked up at the stairs, lined with more photos, a timeline of their childhoods on full display, the memories as sweet as the pie that was waiting for her in the kitchen.

Her grandmother was just setting the coffee to brew when Carly walked into the kitchen, which was dark but cozy at this hour but would be bright and cheerful come the morning. The baker's rack was filled with the pie dishes and cake stands that her grandmother collected, each one unique, many telling a story, like the pink ruffle-edge pie dish that Nana received on her first Mother's Day, from her own mother. Tucked inside was a recipe for one of her grandmother's most secret recipes.

That recipe became what Sunrise Bakery fondly called "Mother's Day Pie." It was only sold on that one Sunday each May but orders were taken weeks in advance. Nana always smiled when she handed over each handmade creation, knowing that half the mothers in town would be enjoying her own mother's recipe.

"That's how she lives on," Nana always told Carly and her sisters, her eyes always glistening.

Now Carly blinked back tears, thinking of her own mother, who prided herself on raising three strong daughters, patiently teaching them to bake. How Nana had made a lemon tart the day that she heard about her daughter's cancer diagnosis, saying that when life sends you something sour, you have to turn it into something sweet.

After Carly's mother died, that bakery had been the only thing that kept Nana going, other than her three granddaughters. She relied on hard work. The routine. And the smiling faces of the community who stopped in each day, bringing a little cheer to their lives.

It was one thing for Nana to take a step back, but to give the bakery away to strangers?

"Soup?" Nana asked, but Carly shook her head.

Her grandmother's smile was rueful. "Straight to dessert. If you were little, I'd have to scold you."

"Ah, but you'd be secretly pleased." Carly admired the pie that was cooling on a rack on the counter. The edges were evenly crimped, and the lattice top was expertly spaced.

Nana cut them each a proper eighth of the pie and plated each slice perfectly. A trick she'd taught Carly at an early age was that you had to cut two slices to free up the first. Carly managed to smile now, surprised that she even remembered that, considering she hadn't baked a pie in well over ten years, not that she'd be admitting that. Cookies and brownies and bar treats were easier to share with her coworkers, and she did, often.

They waited until the coffee was brewed and poured, and cream and sugar added to their liking, before settling in at the table.

"So, tell me everything! How long are you here for? What brings you back?"

The last question was loaded, especially in light of recent news, so Carly started with the easier topic. "I'm here for a couple of weeks, if that's okay." She knew it might take her the length of her entire deadline to come up with a new strategy for her article.

"Okay? That's more than okay!" Instantly, her grandmother's face was replaced by a frown. "Is everything all right in Philly?"

Carly managed a reassuring smile, even though her stomach tightened at the mere mention of her job. How could she say it was anything but wonderful when it was her excuse for staying away all these years and not coming back after college to work in the bakery?

"Just fine. My job is actually part of the reason for my visit. I'm writing a feature about—" She took a bite of pie to stall. "Small towns."

It was true. At least partially.

"Well, isn't that perfect! Hope Hollow is the quintessential small town. Nowhere else most people here would rather live. Well, except those with big city dreams."

Carly rolled her eyes playfully. "I don't have big city dreams. I just...prefer to live in the city."

That was true, at least at first. Once the city had been exciting, a chance for her to carve her own path, instead of following the one planned for her. One that allowed her to start fresh, with no mistakes—or hurt.

But the novelty had worn off, and the days became routine. And now she didn't really know what she wanted; she just knew that she wanted more than what she currently had.

"Any news to share?" Nana looked hopeful, probably wondering about Carly's nonexistent love life.

"Nothing other than work."

Nana shook her head sadly. "You know you work too much."

"I wonder where I got it from?" Carly gave her grandmother a pointed look. "And work isn't exciting to talk about. Certainly not as interesting as all news around here. Selling the bakery, Nana? But how?"

"How not?" Her grandmother's shoulders sagged a little when she set her fork down. Her trim figure was maintained by never finishing her own desserts, but Carly couldn't resist.

Scooping another forkful into her mouth, she said, "But you said you'd never share our secret recipes with anyone outside of the family."

"That's true, and I won't." Nana sighed. "The recipes would be the company's."

Carly blinked, thinking that she'd been naive in assuming that this day couldn't get any worse. "You mean like a franchise? A chain?"

Already she was picturing their sweet yellow-and-white-striped aprons replaced with something bright and solid, maybe paired with a baseball cap bearing the store's name in a corporate font.

That wasn't the kind of bakery that her editor was expecting her to feature in her article. And it wasn't the type of bakery the residents of Hope Hollow would appreciate either.

"But people have been coming to Sunrise Bakery for generations. What about the Sunday morning muffins? Or the Christmas bread?" Each year, it was prepared in a different shape for the season. The girls had always enjoyed tossing around ideas on Thanksgiving when preparation for the next holiday began.

"Jill and Becca have been on their own for a while now. I don't think they enjoy it as much as they used to. And you know they enjoyed it more than you ever did," her grandmother added.

"Nana." Carly's voice felt as hollow as it did small. She wanted to apologize, to explain, but her grandmother was giving her one of her smiles that showed she understood. Her sisters might not, but at least one person did.

"You're your own person with your own interests and needs. You know that I'd never have wanted you to do anything other than follow your heart."

But Carly hadn't done that, had she? Instead, she'd run from it, broken and beaten as it might have been. She'd left this town, the bakery, everyone and everything she'd ever loved, and started over.

And now she'd come back. And she had the horrible feeling that she was too late.

three

Sunrise Bakery was given its name for a reason, and long before Carly came along with her big smile and sunny disposition.

It had been ten years since Carly had woken up before five, and after snoozing her alarm three times, she finally tossed back the quilt on her childhood bed and flicked on the bedside light, bringing the soft pink painted walls to light. She smiled as she dressed and quickly pulled her hair back, her heart softening that after all these years, Nana had left the row of mismatched pillows and stuffed animals along the window seat that overlooked the back garden.

But then, that was Nana. Always preserving the past.

A lump grew in Carly's throat when she thought of the bakery being sold. Nana might be putting on a brave face, but that was only because she felt she had to be the strong one. And because she thought she had no choice.

Downstairs, Carly was surprised to see her grandmother

was already awake and enjoying a cup of coffee on the sun porch.

"Old habits die hard?" she asked, poking her head around the open French door and looking inside the small room with furniture faded by the natural light.

Her grandmother looked up in surprise. "I could say the same! I figured you'd be sleeping until at least eight on your vacation."

This trip was far from a vacation, but Carly didn't have time to get into details. She had a new plan, and she didn't have time to waste.

"I thought I'd go over to the bakery and offer up my help. It's the least I can do while I'm here."

Her grandmother's look of appreciation told Carly just how much this meant.

"What do you have going on today?" she asked, wondering if she should perhaps spend the day with Nana instead.

But her grandmother just grinned and said, "Plenty. Besides, it will do you good to spend some quality time with your sisters."

"I could always come back early." If she wasn't asked to leave first. Carly recalled her final summer here in Hope Hollow when she couldn't wait to end her shift and jump into Nick's car, which was usually waiting out front. Nana could only shake her head at the romantic distraction, but Jill hadn't been shy in voicing her feelings on the matter. Or that Carly's help wasn't really helpful at all.

"As I said, I have plenty going on! Especially when I

didn't know you were coming. Had I known, I would have cleared my schedule!"

Carly didn't know if this was her grandmother's way of telling her that the bakery was where she was needed or if Nana really did have plans. She was popular in town. Beloved, really. Which just made the thought of losing the family business all the more heartbreaking.

"If you're sure…"

"I'll see you tonight then?" Nana's eyes were questioning as if she wasn't quite sure that Carly would still be here later on.

Carly nodded. She would. And who knew, maybe by tonight she'd manage to convince her sisters that selling the bakery was no longer up for discussion.

That's what she hoped, but even she knew that wasn't very realistic. She took the car into town instead of walking, eager to get there, and parked behind the building, where two SUVs she recognized as belonging to her sisters already sat, side by side. Both were ivory in color; both were relatively new. Really, could things be that tight?

But then she remembered that her sisters ran deliveries. The cars were probably bought together, for more than personal reasons. And she was just being touchy because that's what being here was doing to her. Bringing back feelings that were long buried, like the way Jill and Becca always seemed joined at the hip, leaving her always trying to catch up until she stopped trying.

Like the way her stomach still swooped when she thought of Nick Sutton.

Nick. Back in town. And handsome as ever, she thought, pushing the image of his face from her mind.

She parked beside one of the twin vehicles and walked to the back door, surprising both of her sisters when she walked directly into the kitchen. Jill was rolling out pie crust and Becca was scooping muffin mixture into tins.

"Don't look so happy to see me," Carly joked. She plucked an apron from the pantry drawer where they kept fresh ones in stock. "The least I can do is make myself useful while I'm here."

She'd be useful, all right. Useful enough to turn this bakery around. To remind her sisters that this was a family business with family recipes and that it would probably be better to shutter the doors completely than to sell out.

Selling the business was like giving away a piece of their family history. The very soul that had started this place.

"Here," Becca said, wiping her hands on her apron. "Why don't you finish up these muffins? You just need to put them in the oven for—"

"I know how long." Carly gave her sister a pointed look. She may no longer work here, but that didn't mean she'd forgotten the basics. They were ingrained in her as deeply as the stories Nana used to tell when she rolled out pie dough.

"And don't use the bottom oven. It needs to be serviced. The timer stopped working and there's something off with the temperature."

"Yes, ma'am," Carly replied.

"There's more batter behind you," Becca said, giving her a small smile.

Jill began breaking eggs into a large mixing bowl. Even if

she hadn't seen it, Carly would have known from the time of day that she was making her morning quiche. The doors to the storefront would open at seven, which was early for many, but perfect for the mothers who sneaked in a quick run before they had to get their kids ready for the day, or workers who stole a little fresh air before they had to sit behind a desk all afternoon. Weekends were especially busy, but those were the mornings that the family doubled down, producing Danishes and scones, and coffee cakes that some people bought whole instead of by the slice.

They worked in silence for about five minutes until Carly decided that both of her sisters were waiting for her to mention her errand last night.

"It would have been nice if one of you had told me that Nick Sutton was back in town." She filled the muffin tin with large scoops of batter, careful to keep them even.

Now the silence was no longer so comfortable. Not surprisingly, it was Becca who broke it.

"I tried to tell you last night." Her expression looked pained, and Carly almost felt ashamed. Becca knew heartbreak just as much as she did. If not more, given that she'd been engaged when her relationship a couple of years ago.

"You were the one who said you couldn't take any more bad news," Jill jumped in.

It was true. But could she classify Nick being back in town as bad news?

It certainly wasn't good news.

"Well, a little warning might have been nice. Although, I'm not sure who was more surprised. Me or him. The only one who didn't seem phased was

Frankie, who couldn't be parted from his plate of spaghetti, so he sat and listened to the entire awkward exchange."

Becca gave a small laugh and then held up a hand. "Sorry. It's just that I can almost picture it."

"The part about Frankie or the part about colliding with the first guy to break my heart?"

The only guy, really.

"Both?" Becca winced.

"I'm glad my romantic history is so amusing." Carly pursed her lips, but she couldn't exactly be mad at her sisters. Not about this, at least.

She filled another muffin tin, popped it in the top oven, and set the timer. Two tins were already cooling on the rack —chocolate chip, yum—and she pulled a basket from the shelf, knowing they were ready to be transferred to the bakery case.

"Thanks," Jill said, sounding surprised.

"I told you that I'm here to help," Carly said. And she was, just maybe not in the way that she was directly implying.

She had an article to write and a little more than two more weeks to get it into her editor's hands, polished and complete with photos to boot, or she could kiss any chance of that promotion goodbye for good.

If she didn't have to say goodbye to this bakery first.

~

The morning crowd was always the busiest, and the regular faces were a welcome sight—and a reminder that this bakery was worth fighting for, and not just for the Parker family.

"Why, it's our little ray of sunshine!" Mr. Quincy beamed when he saw Carly behind the counter and she did the same in return. The old widower lived next door to Nana's house and asked her out for dinner at least once a month, always smiling and promising to try again when she turned him down. He was nearly as stubborn as Nana, not that it was helping either one of them in this case.

Despite the nickname, which she'd grown out of when she turned thirteen and found downright embarrassing, Carly smiled.

"Mr. Quincy. Your usual?"

"You remember?" His eyes went wide behind his wire-framed glasses.

"Black coffee and raspberry Danish?" She hoped now that he hadn't decided to finally mix things up after all these years and get adventurous enough to try a blueberry muffin. Mr. Quincy was a creature of habit if there ever was one, which meant he was probably still asking out Nana, and still promising to come knocking again four weeks later.

His face melted into a shy smile. "You did remember. And this is exactly what brings me back here every day. Sure, the food is as good as it gets, but it's that personal touch. You can only find it in Hope Hollow."

Carly didn't disagree with him as she pulled a pair of tongs from the counter and slid the best raspberry Danish into a white paper bag.

"Is that the only thing?" She gave a knowing lift of her eyebrow and Mr. Quincy grinned a little broader.

"It's disappointing not seeing Sharon here each morning," he admitted, referring to Nana. "She was certainly a perk to my day. Although, I'm guessing having you back is a perk to hers."

"And mine," Carly said.

"Life in the city must be a lot different than here in this little town."

Carly caught his eye, which bore the glint of an ulterior motive, and gave a polite smile as she filled a to-go cup with strong coffee. She considered asking him about how his grandson was enjoying Los Angeles, but any reference to Jonah would only make her think of the way he'd broken Becca's heart. That was hardly poor Mr. Quincy's fault.

"It's certainly nice to be back," she said, handing everything over.

"Back to stay then?" His tone was so hopeful, she almost hated to disappoint him. He seemed to be reaching for something—hope that his own family member would return perhaps.

Or have a change of heart.

"I'll be here for another two weeks," she said. But now she couldn't help but worry about what the next two weeks would bring.

Luckily, the flow in and out of the bakery was enough to keep her mind off her troubles, and by the time the morning rush had slowed down and then the lunch crowd left, she was finally able to catch her breath.

"I don't know how you do this every day," she confided to Becca.

"It's not usually this busy," Becca admitted. She gave Carly a pointed look. "Word of your return must have circulated."

"I guess I'm good for business then!" Carly laughed, but Becca just frowned a little and went back to work.

Her sister didn't pause from wiping the crumbs off the counter. "You are. And I'm thankful for it. Besides, I don't know how you sit all day behind a desk staring at a computer."

They grinned at each other.

"Fair point," Carly said. It wasn't a secret that she hadn't loved working at the bakery as much as her sisters. She did it, and she was even good at it, but she'd always felt like she was being told what to do, ordered around by two older sisters and a grandmother and mother who all had a say in things.

"By four, I'm usually ready to lock the door, though," Becca admitted with a conspiratorial wink.

Was that really how Becca felt? Was she counting the days or weeks until she didn't have to be here at all? And what would she do then?

Carly knew she could ask, but she wasn't sure that she was ready to hear the answer.

Instead, she checked her watch. It was nearly three. A quick glance at the display case showed that the breakfast items had been cleared out, and other than half a raspberry pie, some brownies, and a variety of cookies, the only thing they had to offer was coffee and tea.

"There won't be much left for donation tonight," Carly

said, allowing her mind to slip over to last night's visit at the firehouse.

Becca gave her a knowing look and set the rag on the counter. "No drop-offs tonight anyway. We'll probably sell out, which isn't always a good thing. If we sell out before four, I'm always left wondering if we didn't make enough." She shrugged. "I guess we won't have to worry about these things much longer. But I do hate the thought of not giving back to the community."

"What do you mean?" Carly asked.

"If we sell—"

Carly cringed at this word and Becca even seemed to take pause.

"The franchise can't donate the leftovers. They have policies and procedures."

"Policies and procedures? Becca, is this seriously what you want? To see this bakery replaced with generic logos and factory-made food?"

"What I want doesn't really seem to matter. We don't always get what we want." Becca's smile was gone from her eyes and Carly knew she wasn't just thinking about the bakery. She was thinking about her fiancé. Ex-fiancé. About the wedding she'd planned, the dress she'd never worn.

The cake that had never been baked.

"Anyway, I'd better get back to the kitchen and see if Jill needs any help," Becca said, shaking off the hurt in her voice and replacing it with a bright smile.

Carly understood. There were some heartbreaks that were easier to forget than talk about.

"Are you going to be fine out here for a bit longer?" Becca asked.

"Of course!" Carly was insulted that her sister would even have to ask, like she was a volunteer, not a member of the family, but then she supposed that Becca had a point. Carly hadn't been a part of this business in a long time.

She was an outsider. And now more than ever, her voice might not matter.

She busied herself with rearranging the items in the display case when the bell over the door jangled and a little girl with long brown hair walked in and straight up to the counter.

"Hello," Carly greeted her with the same smile she gave each customer, but she did flick her gaze to the door, to see if the child's mother was following.

"I'll have my usual, please." The child's large dark eyes were earnest as they blinked at hers. Then, seeming to realize that Carly might not know what she meant, she said, "An oatmeal cookie."

"My favorite," Carly confided with a grin. "For here or to go?"

"For here." The little girl gave an expectant smile.

Interesting. No mother. Granted, the Hope Hollow School was just around the corner and some of the older kids liked to stop by for a treat in the afternoon. Carly could still remember starting her shift on those afternoons only to see some of the boys she'd crushed on standing behind the counter. Namely, Nick Sutton, whom she'd eyed long before he'd ever noticed her.

Nick always ordered...an oatmeal cookie.

Carly reached for a small plate and placed a cookie on top.

"Becca always gives me a glass of milk," the little girl whispered, cupping the side of her mouth.

"Oh." Carly nodded a few times. "Okay. Of course! So you're a regular around here, then. I'm Becca's sister."

"Little sister," Becca's voice said from behind. Carly caught the groan of the kitchen door swinging closed at the end of the room. "I see you've met Daisy."

"Unofficially," Carly said. "Hello, Daisy. I'm Carly."

"For the after-school crowd." Becca handed Carly a basket of brownies cut into four-inch squares. The smell of chocolate was so strong that Carly took a moment just to enjoy it.

Becca seemed to hesitate for a moment and then went back into the kitchen, leaving Carly to add the brownies to the display case.

"Let me get you that milk," she said to Daisy. It wasn't something they usually offered, only on request, and usually to kids. She pulled a carton from the mini fridge under the counter, where they kept the cream for the lattes.

"Are you on your own today?" Carly guessed the little girl was somewhere around nine or ten judging from the pink unicorn backpack she carried.

"Just until four." Daisy was fumbling with the front pocket of her bag. "Becca never lets me pay, but my dad said that if she doesn't, I should still put this in the tip jar."

"Your dad sounds like a really thoughtful guy," Carly said.

Now the little girl's eyes lit up and she beamed. "He's the best."

Daisy took her milk and cookie and carefully carried them over to a seat near the window, where she settled onto the chair and enjoyed her snack. Carly watched her for a moment, realizing by how comfortable she was here that this was a fairly regular occurrence, but then the boys with their bags slung over one shoulder appeared through the window and a moment later the bell jingled and soon she was handing out brownies until the basket was empty. The cookie basket, too.

She checked her watch to see it was nearly four. Closing time, however unofficially, because Nana was never one to kick anyone out. And of course, there was no way that she could send Daisy out the door.

Carly smiled as she filled another glass with milk and set one of the remaining oatmeal cookies on a napkin. She walked around the counter and approached Daisy.

"I thought you could use a refill," she said.

The little girl's smile widened when she looked to the door, which jingled another arrival.

Carly turned, expecting to see some preteen school girls she'd have to disappoint by telling them they were fresh out of brownies, but instead, she came face to face with Nick Sutton. Again.

"Nick." Her voice seemed to lodge in her throat. Running into him at the fire station was one thing, but did he actually think it was acceptable to come into the bakery?

For a moment, she indulged herself by thinking that he might be seeking her out, but that fantasy was interrupted when Daisy cried, "Daddy!" and jumped out of the chair, bumping Carly's legs in the process, and then flung her arms around her father.

Her father.

Carly felt like the air had come out of her lungs. She knew about the baby all those years ago. It was the entire reason for her heartache. The only way that she couldn't exactly hate him. Nick was, at the end of the day, a good man. A good man who had done what they both knew was the right thing.

Even if it had felt so wrong.

"I see you've met my daughter." He raised his eyebrows.

"Your daughter!" Carly's voice was unnaturally high and she felt like she was smiling like a maniac.

Now she wondered how she hadn't seen it. The deep-set eyes. Even the warm shade of brown hair. She'd never met the woman that Nick had dated in college and broken up with shortly before their summer romance, but Daisy was all Nick.

"You know my daddy?" Daisy looked at her in wonder. "How?"

Carly glanced at Nick, who seemed to be as lost for words as she was. She managed a tight smile and said, "Oh, everyone in Hope Hollow knows each other. And I grew up here. Your Daddy and I knew each other when we were younger."

She couldn't look him in the eyes, so instead, she turned around and reached for a white paper bag on the nearby counter. "Here, Daisy, why don't you slide that cookie in here? Maybe you can save it for later. Or share it with your...dad."

This was all too much. Why hadn't she considered last night that by seeing Nick, she'd probably see his wife and daughter too?

The blood seemed to drain from her face for a moment and she all but crammed the cookie into the bag. Was the woman Nick left her for about to come through that door, too?

"My cookie," Nick teased as he reached for the bag before Daisy could snatch it, resulting in a fit of giggles from his daughter.

His daughter. For so long it had just felt like an idea. A reason for why things had ended between them.

Now it was a reality. And Carly had to admit, it was a beautiful one.

She felt her shoulders relax but only a little. She felt like an outsider, observing a family dynamic that she wasn't part of, but once wished she had been.

It was a familiar feeling, one she'd experienced a lot recently.

"Well, I should probably get Daisy home," Nick said, even when he made no show of moving.

Home. Carly could practically picture it now. A warmly lit house, family photos lining the wall. A happy trio gathered around the table, sharing parts of their day over a homemade dinner.

Nick was grinning at his daughter, and the smile didn't fade when he looked back at her.

Carly realized with the full impact that came almost as a

shock that he was happy, and not just happy in the moment, no, genuinely, thoroughly happy.

Happy with his life. Happy with his choice all those years ago.

She pushed back a wave of sadness. It was for the best, she thought, looking fondly at the little girl. It had all turned out for the best for him.

But not, she thought, for her.

"We're closing up soon anyway," she said. Things were quieting down, and the only people who would stop by were those looking for a last-minute dessert purchase before dinner.

"It was good seeing you again," Nick said, gazing at her so steadily that she struggled to hold his stare.

Carly wiped the crumbs off the table where Daisy had been sitting and collected the plate and half-finished glass of milk.

"Seems to be a daily occurrence," she joked, but her laugh felt high-pitched and nervous. Would this be a daily thing? She wasn't sure she could take two more weeks of it. Especially now, knowing that the next time, he could easily be holding hands with the woman he left her to marry.

"That's small-town life for you." Nick took Daisy's hand. "Well, we'd better get home."

Carly managed to nod and even wave goodbye, watching for longer than she should have as they walked down the street, and then disappeared out of view. Of course, Nick had somewhere to be. A home. A family.

And she had nothing but an empty apartment waiting for her in Philly.

four

The evening brought a chill with it and Carly shivered when she and Becca stepped outside onto Main Street. They'd stayed late prepping for tomorrow, making sure to avoid sensitive topics and instead catching each other up on their lives. Carly omitted the part about her article and the upcoming promotion. Now, both seemed as far-fetched as keeping Sunrise Bakery in the family.

Becca locked the bakery door with her key and dropped it back into her tote, but not before giving Carly a sly look. "I see you met Nick's daughter today."

"Again," Carly said to Becca. "A little warning might have been nice."

The bakery was closed, and what little there was left to do Jill had volunteered to take care of so that Becca could enjoy her monthly book club meeting. Carly saw it as a recognition on their older sister's part that it was important for Becca to fill her free time with new activities since her engagement had ended.

"Sorry," Becca said, and her tone showed she meant it. "I didn't see an opportunity."

"Well, I found out soon enough." Carly glanced in the shop windows as they walked down Main Street, feeling relaxed at the familiar sites of her youth even when a part of her chest still ached when she thought of Nick.

Everyone had one that got away. The romance that might have been.

Becca knew it best, or at least, the deepest. Thinking of her sister's broken engagement to a man she'd dated for years, Carly felt like she had no room to talk and certainly no business still licking her wounds over something that had ended ten years ago. Her relationship with Nick was short-lived. Interrupted before it barely had a chance to begin.

Being back here stirred things up. Made her think of times gone by, memories that she'd thought she'd forgotten.

Ones, she realized, she'd hoped to forget.

She wondered how Becca did it. Living here day after day, reminded of the man she loved, even if she didn't have to look at him. Working in the bakery where their mother once stood, feeling her absence every time she entered that kitchen.

"You and Nick seemed to get along though." Becca looked at her hesitantly, and at this, Carly burst out laughing.

"You were watching us through the kitchen door window, weren't you?"

Becca gave a guilty shrug, but she didn't look one bit sorry. "Just...looking out for you."

Now that, Carly believed. But she also knew that when it

came to gossip, no one in this town could particularly resist. Probably, she couldn't either.

"What happened between Nick and me was years ago. He moved on. So did I. Literally."

"Yes, but now you're both back."

And he had a child. A family.

And Carly didn't even have a cat.

"I'm only here for a visit. Besides, what Nick and I had was just a summer romance." Only that wasn't true, only technically. Their relationship may have started Memorial Day weekend and ended by Labor Day, but what they had couldn't be lumped into the summer fling category. It had been love. Tried and true. But not meant to be.

It had started as early as her first piano lesson in the Suttons' living room. She'd begged Nana to let her have lessons, and Nana finally obliged, only because she said she was tired of the piano in her living room collecting dust.

Nick was three years older than Carly and in the same grade as Becca, so she'd only vaguely seen him around school, but when he came in the front door that afternoon after her first lesson, barely looking in her direction and asking his mother what was for dinner, she was a goner.

Over time, they became friendly, but he never showed her any real interest. That came later. After he'd left for college, but not before she'd given up hope.

No, that part had come later.

They had three perfect months together the summer she was eighteen, high school behind her, college on the horizon. They filled the days going to the lake, splashing in the water, or just spreading towels out on the sand, talking about everything and nothing all at once, until eventually their dreams seemed to morph and they were talking about future events —school breaks, next summer, what would happen when Nick graduated. How he might move to Philadelphia where she'd be starting school in the fall.

They rode bikes and spent rainy afternoons watching old movies on the couch, laughing at the funny ones, crying at the sad ones. Kissing every chance they had. Every touch felt exciting and new. Every day was full of possibilities.

And then it ended. Nick's college girlfriend—his ex-girlfriend—was pregnant. She thought he should know. And Nick thought he should stand by her.

And the rest was ancient history. Or it should be. But right now, it felt like everywhere Carly turned, Nick and his life were in her face.

That was Hope Hollow for you. You couldn't escape your past. No matter how hard you tried.

Only in the case of the Parkers, you could, Carly supposed, sell it.

"So I guess you wouldn't be interested in hearing any more details about Nick then?" Becca arched an eyebrow and it was clear from the little smile twisting her mouth that there was more she wanted to share.

"Only if you are about to tell me that his wife is approaching us so I have time to turn around and run." Carly laughed, but she wasn't joking. What she and Nick had shared was a summer romance but that didn't mean it hadn't hurt—a lot—when he ultimately chose another woman over her.

Deep down, Carly knew it was the honorable decision,

the right one. That he needed to try to make it work. He owed it to her. To the child. To himself.

And it took everything in her not to point to herself and ask where she fit into this, if she mattered at all.

But there was no room for Carly in that equation. Not then. Certainly not now.

"It's just Nick and Daisy," Becca said.

Now Carly stopped walking for a moment, letting this sink.

"No one knows the full story, but from what we gathered, Nick had a brief marriage, and then his wife left him. Left them both, actually. I think she's only visited that little girl a handful of times in all the years since Nick moved back to Hope Hollow. I've never met her," Becca added, knowing that Carly would be curious.

"That's...terrible." Carly couldn't help but have compassion for that bright-eyed little girl she'd slipped the extra cookie to earlier in the day. "Daisy seems like such a great kid."

"Oh, Daisy's a sweetheart." Becca smiled now.

Carly swallowed hard and focused on the sidewalk for a moment. Nick. A single father. How had that happened? And why did she even care? She could tell herself it was because she'd met Daisy, worried about her welfare, even though the child seemed very well-adjusted and loved. But the truth was that a part of her still cared about Nick. About more than his welfare.

"And Nick?"

Becca seemed to consider this for a moment. She punched the crosswalk sign and they waited for the light to switch. "At first he seemed quiet, but then it was probably strange being back when he'd been gone so long. But once he settled in, he seemed relaxed. Like he'd never left."

"This town has a way of doing that. Making it feel like you'd never left." Or maybe, wish you never had. Carly's heart pulled tight when she thought of how much was changing, though. How much had happened in her absence.

"Is he…"

"Seeing anyone?" Becca slid her a glance before she hopped off the curb. Carly hurried to catch up with her as they crossed the street. "I think some of the guys at the station have set him up but nothing's really panned out. His entire life is that little girl."

Carly let that sink in, but like so many things, it would take time to digest.

"So she comes into the bakery after school when Nick's at the station."

"Only if her grandparents can't watch her, and he's arranged most of his shifts to work around her schedule. Nick's mom still teaches piano, and his father hasn't retired yet." Becca's chin lifted a notch as they passed the wood-sided church where she'd once planned to be married.

Carly watched as Becca kept her eyes in front of her. The knuckles of the hand that gripped her handbag straps were white.

"I guess you can't outrun your past," Carly murmured, even though she wasn't directly talking about her own situation.

Becca's smile was wan. Jonah hadn't just broken off their engagement, he'd also ditched town. Carly wondered if

Becca kept tabs on him, but it was a sensitive topic and she didn't want to press. If Becca wanted to say anything about it, she would.

"But what about our past? Our business? There has to be a way to keep things going." Carly considered telling her sister about the article, about how it might help the bakery if they could just stick things out a little longer, but Becca just heaved a sigh.

"Nothing lasts forever, Carly. Life is always evolving and changing and it's better to move with it. Nothing good comes from clinging to something that you can't hold on to, not when you've put up a good fight."

But had they? Carly wasn't so sure.

"And who knows, maybe we won't come to terms for the sale," Becca said.

Carly felt her heart flutter with hope, but her head told her to be careful. To guard her heart. Not selling wasn't the same as keeping the bakery.

"Well, I'm in town for another two weeks, and I'm going to be there. Every day. Like before."

"That will be nice," Becca said, but her eyes looked tired and sad. "Like old times. It will be…good to remember it like that."

Carly bit back a wave of frustration. Of her two sisters, she was closest to Becca, and not just in age. She could always tell Becca anything, knowing that Becca had a special way of understanding, whereas Jill was more stoic and certainly less emotional. She was like Nana in that sense, too.

"You sound so resigned," Carly observed.

Becca looked a little guilty. "I guess I am. There was a lot of thought that led up to this decision. It wasn't easy, and it still isn't."

"I guess I'm just holding out hope." Even though more and more it felt like denial.

Becca grinned broadly. "Good! I knew I could count on you for that."

"So you don't really want to sell the bakery?" Carly asked carefully.

"Of course I don't!" Becca shook her head as if Carly should have known better than to even ask. But she didn't know better. She felt like she didn't know her sisters at all. That she had been excluded from a major decision. One that she might not have a vote in, and maybe that was fair given how long she'd been away.

"Good," Carly said. She pulled in a breath and let it out. Tomorrow she'd talk to Jill. Maybe her grandmother again too. She could tell them about the article, and how it could change everything for the better.

That maybe it was just what they needed, and somehow she'd known it, deep down, which was why she'd pitched the idea in the first place.

That somehow, she was still a part of that bakery, too.

They'd covered two blocks by the time Carly felt a little better, and she realized in surprise that they were already near Becca's destination.

"Tanya's house is just two doors down," Becca said, pointing out a little cottage with a yellow front door flanked by two pots of multi-colored tulips. The only thing that could have made it sweeter was if it had window boxes, too.

"You're thinking the house would be even cuter with window boxes, aren't you?" Becca asked.

Carly looked at her sharply and then laughed. "How did you know?"

"Because I know you, Carly. And I know how much you love window boxes on houses. You always said you'd have them when you grew up."

Had she? Carly blinked now, trying to remember a time when she'd envisioned a future, certainly one that wasn't anything like the life she was living.

But then it came to her: she and Nick, on side-by-side towels down at the lake, looking far into the future, after Carly would have graduated. This town wasn't so bad, they'd both said, and by then they'd both have had their stints in the city. Besides, Hope Hollow was what bonded them. This community, this history. It was all Carly had ever known then, and all she really wanted.

They'd have a simple life. A sweet little house. One with flowers that would somehow grow better than all the ones she'd attempted in the past.

One with window boxes.

She shook those thoughts away. "I don't even have a balcony at my apartment, and my windows face an alley."

"It's not too late," Becca said knowingly.

Carly stared at her, wondering what Becca meant by that. Never too late to add window boxes to a rental apartment that faced the back of a neighboring building and, down below, garbage dumpsters?

Or never too late to move back? To live the life she'd once dreamed of having.

Hoped to have.

"Ah but it is," she said, remaining vague. "And I should probably get home to Nana."

"She has bridge club tonight," Becca said. "She won't be done for a few hours."

"Oh." Carly didn't know what disappointed her more, that her grandmother wasn't at the house right now or that she didn't know the simple things like her grandmother's social plans.

And that she had no one to blame but herself. And her choices. To move away from this town and distance herself from all the parts of the past that had once meant so much to her and still did.

"You can come in if you'd like," Becca told her. "Unless you want to go back to the house and listen to a bunch of old ladies getting feisty with each other. You know how seriously Nana takes her card games."

Carly laughed. She did. She taught the girls to play at an early age, how to order their hands and hold them close. She didn't let them win, even when Carly was only about seven or eight and was just learning the rules. And she kept a poker face, even if they were just playing Go Fish.

"I haven't read the book!" she said to her sister.

Becca shrugged. "Neither did I."

They both laughed and Carly thought about it for a split second. It would be nice to step inside, have a glass of wine, and maybe even catch up with some old classmates. She hadn't even seen Joanna yet—maybe her oldest friend would be inside.

"Okay," she said, "You convinced me."

Not that it took much. She enjoyed her sister's company. So much so that she wondered how she'd gone without it for so long.

Evenings, when he wasn't on shift, were busy, and the time he looked forward to most all week—other than weekends. On Fridays, he and Daisy usually ordered a pizza and watched a movie, or played a game. Sometimes they went bowling—the fire station had a league, and he was the worst player on it because he was one of the only guys who didn't practice in his free time.

But that was okay. His priority was his daughter. Watching her laugh, helping her with homework, and just enjoying her company.

She'd always been his priority. Every decision he made with her in mind. So why did he feel like he'd still managed to mess it all up?

The phone rang, and Nick glanced at the screen, frowning when he saw the name lighting up in bold letters.

He glanced at his daughter, who was happily engrossed in a movie she'd already seen twice, and whispered to her that he'd be right back. He slipped into the study and closed the pocket door behind him before he connected the call.

"Liz," he said. His heart was thumping, because anything that involved Daisy made him worried.

"I wasn't sure you'd answer," his ex-wife responded lightly. There was traffic in the background and their connection wasn't very strong, meaning that she was far away, distracted. Meaning the call would be brief.

"Daisy and I were just settling in for a movie. I can pause it and go get her." Daisy would happily trade the movie for a talk with her mother, but given the tone of Liz's voice, he worried that the call would be short, leaving Daisy disappointed and their fun Friday night ruined.

"Actually, tonight I wanted to talk to you."

"Oh?" Nick couldn't think of what was left to say. They'd hashed it out, over the years, all the little things and the big things. All the reasons why they should break up and all the reasons they should stick it out. What they wanted, what they didn't. Why they were so unhappy.

Eventually, work became an excuse to avoid these types of conversations—and each other. He was just as guilty of it as she was: working long hours, climbing the corporate ladder, and trying to convince himself that what he was doing mattered even though his heart only felt full when he saw his daughter's smile. And even that wasn't very often.

At home, he and Liz took to disappearing to their own corners of the city apartment, or tag teaming outings with Daisy, each citing work as an excuse to let the other take a turn.

In the end, it was Liz who had the final word, telling them she'd taken a job in Seattle. She needed to start over. She needed to "find out who she was."

In other words, goodbye.

Nick could still feel the swell of anger now, the same as that night, three years ago. He'd stood there, staring at the woman he'd grown to care for but, if he was being honest, probably never really loved.

Liz sent cards and lavish gifts to Daisy to make up for everything she missed. She visited for their first Christmas in Hope Hollow, staying exactly one night, and then again the next year for Daisy's birthday. Since then, they'd seen her an odd weekend here or there.

"I've been thinking of visiting. Soon."

He nodded then forced himself to say, "Sure. Of course. When were you thinking?" He'd never keep Daisy from her mother. Daisy loved Liz, and not just because she came bearing toys and stuffed animals, princess wands, and other expensive items her demanding job could afford.

"I have some time off in a couple of weeks. I was thinking I might stay a bit longer this time. I've missed Daisy." Liz's voice sounded sad, not just far away, and Nick clenched his jaw, refusing to feel sorry for her. She'd made her choice. They both had—several along the way.

"Well, I'm sure Daisy will like that. She has school, of course."

"Of course. But a break is coming up?"

Had she actually checked Daisy's school website for the calendar? Nick managed not to state the obvious, which was that she hadn't been there for any of Daisy's school events— not the classroom nights or the holiday pageants, not the teacher conferences or the birthday lunches, or the end-of- school-year picnics which he volunteered at, every June. No, she was paying attention to the calendar because it benefited her. It gave her a chance to slide into town, have a little fun, and then check back out before the daily responsibility settled in.

"Spring break."

After a pause, Liz said, "Well, keep it open for me."

Nick had been thinking of taking Daisy camping, now that she was old enough. Or maybe into Boston, but maybe not, in case it made her think of their old life, and made her miss her mother.

But now he wouldn't have to worry about that because Liz was coming to town.

And Daisy would put that over a camping trip any day.

"Will do," he said, then cleared his throat and hung up the phone.

Carly was disappointed to see that Joanna was not at the book club meeting, which was only surprising given that she ran the bookstore in town. Carly knew from their monthly phone calls, however, that book clubs sometimes frustrated Joanna when they turned into a social hour and not a serious discussion about the literature she loved so much.

As Becca had implied, it didn't matter that Carly hadn't read the book. Had it not been for the theme of the drinks and snacks (a proper English tea, complete with cucumber sandwiches and Earl Grey-infused cocktails), Carly might have just as well assumed that they had all read Stephen King instead of Jane Austen.

Becca walked over and handed her a glass of white wine. "Having fun?"

"Jill doesn't come to these things?" Carly took a sip. So far, she'd interacted with four of her former classmates, all of whom were engaged, married, or pregnant. And all she had to show for things was a job that she might not hold on to much longer.

"Sometimes," Becca said. Then, after a pause, she added, "But I think she'd rather not have to answer difficult questions, lately. There's plenty of gossip in town about the bakery since Nana retired, as you can imagine."

Carly could. She sipped her drink and watched Becca move over toward a group of friends that Carly remembered from years back, finding it interesting just how many of their classmates had chosen to return to Hope Hollow after college.

But then, why wouldn't they? It was a charming town, filled with pretty shops and storefronts, a good school system, and easy access for a day trip to Boston or even New York. And more than that, there was a community of friends and neighbors.

And family.

Carly didn't realize that she was frowning until she saw one of their old neighbors approach, her expression tentative.

Carly forced herself to relax, to fight the nostalgia that had come out of nowhere, and gave her old playmate an overdue hug.

"It feels like just yesterday we were climbing that old tree in your backyard," she told Erika.

"Now my sons are climbing it," Erika said with a proud smile. She wasted no time in fishing her cell phone from her handbag and pulling up a photo of a toe-headed toddler with a bright smile and a slightly older boy with a mischievous grin.

"They're precious," Carly said, feeling her spirits brighten.

"They certainly keep me busy," Erika admitted. "It's not easy balancing motherhood with a full-time career. I'm selling houses now if you're in the market."

Carly coughed. "No. I'm not here to stay."

"Shame," Erika said. "Now, what about you? How's life in Philly? You must have a lot going on to keep you there."

Carly blinked for a moment, considering Erika's choice of works. For so long, it had been more about what was keeping her away from Hope Hollow. Now, being back, she almost couldn't imagine leaving it all behind again. And as for what was keeping her in Philadelphia...

She realized that there might not be anything keeping her there at all.

five

Carly was still thinking about the bakery long after she'd left it the next day, but before she talked anymore to her sisters, she decided to start with Nana. It wasn't just because she knew she could always talk through anything with her grandmother—Nana may not work at Sunrise Bakery anymore but the way that Carly saw it, it was still her business.

Nana, however, didn't see it that way.

"Your sisters make all the decisions when it comes to that place," Nana said as they walked briskly down the road, past Erika's parents' home, the climbing tree visible from the side yard. Even though Carly had spent the entire day on her feet, she couldn't turn down Nana's invitation for a walk. It was a cool spring day and there wasn't a cloud in the sky. The daffodils were still in bloom but the tulips weren't far behind.

Either, Carly realized, was Mr. Quincy.

She stopped walking to let Mr. Quincy and his dog catch up, a slow endeavor for them both. Trying to push her emotions aside, she crouched down to pet Barney, the chocolate lab that had been downright hyper the last time she'd seen him. Now, his legs were stiff, his coat a little grey, but his brown eyes were still wise and gentle.

She stroked his head and told him he was a good boy.

Nana, however, was not so charmed. She lifted her nose a little in the air while Mr. Quincy smiled at her good-naturedly.

"You must be pleased to have your granddaughter here at long last!" he told her.

Carly tried to fight the sting of his words. His intentions were in the right place. And he wasn't exactly wrong, either. And she knew that he was probably thinking of his grandson, wishing he might return too.

"I'm certainly grateful," Nana remarked, and Carly detected a hint of defense creep into her voice. Her smile seemed forced when she linked arms with Carly and said, "She's keeping me very busy."

Carly resisted the urge to frown. Since her return, she'd spent more time with her sisters than with Nana, and that was partly due to the fact that Nana was so busy with her social calendar—just as she'd said.

"You never were one to sit down or stay still for long." Mr. Quincy gave her a knowing smile and then winked at Carly. "But I haven't given up trying to pin you down. I suppose that dinner is off the table for this weekend, then?"

To the best of Carly's knowledge, Nana had never graced poor Mr. Quincy with an acceptance of his overtures and they'd been coming since Carly was barely a teenager. Mr. Quincy had lost his wife not long before a car accident took his only daughter and her husband, leaving him to finish raising his grandson.

But even a handsome widower didn't appeal to Nana. Long before Mr. Quincy's advances started, Carly's mother used to tease Nana—encourage her to go out and have a little fun. But the more she'd joked, the less Nana had found it amusing.

Now she said, "Oh, I can't possibly part with Carly while she's visiting."

"Another weekend then, perhaps," Mr. Quincy said with a twinkle in his blue eyes.

Nana just gave a little shrug and let them pass to continue on their walk.

Carly waited until Mr. Quincy was out of earshot to say, "Nana, you know he likes you."

"Oh, he's just a flirt," she said with a brush of her hand. "And you know that your grandfather was the only man for me."

Carly gave her a long look. One that she knew Nana understood. Nana's husband had died years before Carly was even born.

"But you've been alone for so many years, Nana."

"Alone?" Nana squeezed her arm tighter. "How can I be alone with three granddaughters? Now come on. Let's go back to the house and have some tea in the garden. I've suddenly lost my desire to take a long walk today."

Carly agreed but only because her feet ached from so much time on them. She'd forgotten that about working in the bakery—she'd forgotten a lot of things, really. How the smell of fresh vanilla scones could warm up the chilliest of mornings, how a slice of cinnamon crumble cake could bring a smile to her lips, however fleeting.

It was all those little moments of happiness that only Sunrise Bakery could bring.

Today, she promised herself, as they made their way back to the house, she would have a good firm chat with Nana.

"Go pick some flowers for me, Carly," Nana said when they entered the front hall. "We can put them on the patio table while we enjoy our tea."

Carly knew that in early April there wouldn't be much to pick from, but she didn't argue. While Nana busied herself filling the kettle in the kitchen, Carly slipped out the back door and surveyed the flower beds that edged the yard.

Frowning at something that caught her eye, she walked a little faster toward the tall row of arborvitae that divided Nana's house from Frannie's—one that Jill always joked had been planted with clear intent. The two women had been neighbors for at least fifteen years but, after delivering a basket of homemade muffins upon Frannie's arrival and later discovering them on top of her trash can the next morning, Nana had held a grudge ever since.

Now, the thick, dense foliage was missing a spot. And not from lack of nourishment, either. Carly inspected it closer and, with a little shock, realized that a perfect hole had been trimmed straight through!

"Nana," Carly called, her heart pounding with indignation as she all but ran back up to the house where her grandmother was stepping out onto the patio with two tea cups. "Are you aware that there is a *hole* in your hedge?"

Nana's eyes flicked across the empty yard before she

whispered, "It's fine. It's fine. Probably just the act of a harmless animal."

Carly stared at her grandmother as understanding set in. "Nana, did you cut this hole yourself?"

"Keep your voice down." Nana gave a little sniff and set the two empty cups on the table, struggling to make eye contact. "I like to keep an eye on things. Neighborhood watch."

"Neighborhood nosy is more like it," Carly said with a laugh. "And it works both ways. Now Frannie can look in on your yard, too!"

"Not if she doesn't know the hole is there," Nana said with a little smile.

"Oh Nana," Carly shook her head, but she was still laughing. "What could possibly be so interesting in Frannie James's backyard?"

"You'd be surprised," Nana said mysteriously. "Life here in Hope Hollow isn't as boring as you might think."

"I never said it was boring," Carly said, feeling more than a little miffed that her grandmother thought she held that opinion.

"Well, it's certainly not as exciting as the city," Nana said lightly. She went back to the kitchen and returned with her teapot, which Carly took from her. Nana settled herself onto one of the garden chairs and motioned for Carly to join her.

Glancing back to make sure that no eyes were appearing on the other side of the hole in the arborvitae, Carly finally went to the table and took her chair. Oh, it felt good to rest these legs.

"I'm sorry that I haven't visited more," Carly said, even

though the person she felt like she was apologizing to was herself. It was painful coming back, just as she'd feared, but not in the way she'd imagined.

Nana's smile was kind. "You have a busy life. And you give me a reason to get out of this town for a bit. I should be thanking you."

But Carly wasn't going to accept her excuse. "I can't help thinking that if I'd stayed that we wouldn't be on the verge of losing the bakery."

"It's a lot more complicated than an extra set of hands," Nana said. "And sometimes love just isn't enough."

Carly nodded. She knew that, the hard way. Anyone who'd lost someone they cared about did.

"But it's not just that," Nana continued, pouring herself some tea. She hesitated for a moment and then set the pot down on the table. "You can't make someone love something they don't."

Carly fell silent because, like most things when it came to her grandmother, there was no sense in arguing. The woman was stubborn. But she was also, usually, right.

After helping her sisters with the Sunday morning rush the next day, Carly decided to stop by the library instead of heading straight back to Nana's. The day was early—Sunrise Bakery had a tradition of closing by noon on Sundays and that at least hadn't changed any more than the recipes over the years—but clouds gathering up ahead made it feel later, and the threat of a rainstorm was a distinct possibility.

Like most buildings in Hope Hollow, the library was old, built in a former schoolhouse, the walls cleared away to make space for shelving. Carly settled herself at a table in the middle of the open space and pulled her laptop from her bag.

Powering up the screen took no time. Finding something to write was another matter. The room was silent, other than the odd turning of a page in the distance or a muffled cough. She could practically feel the ticking of the large clock over the double set of doors, reminding her of the passing of time, the deadline that loomed, not just for her article but for Sunrise Bakery.

Frustrated, she opened a fresh document, this one where she hoped to list ways to keep the bakery in the family, but just as with her article, the page remained as blank as her mind.

"Care if I join you?" a voice interrupted her thoughts.

Carly, still frowning at the screen, barely glanced up when she gave a nod of her head. The table was large and meant to be shared. She just didn't realize whom she had agreed to share it with until she looked up and saw Nick grinning back at her.

She blinked as her face heated, evidence of the way he still affected her. "Nick."

His smile turned rueful. "You didn't realize it was me? I can move if you'd prefer." He made a show of gathering up some books on the table.

She swallowed against the pounding of her heart. "No. No, stay. I mean, no, I didn't realize it was you, but of course, stay."

His grin broadened, reaching his eyes, and bringing out the warmth in them. "Only if you insist."

Now it was her turn to smile. "Now, I wouldn't say that I insist...more that I can't resist."

Immediately, she felt her cheeks flame hotter. Had she just said that? She'd never been able to resist Nick Sutton, that much was true, but what was she doing, flirting with him like this?

He might be single now, but that didn't mean that they could fall back into step where they left off. There was too much distance. Too many years.

Too much pull, she thought, when her chest grew tighter just looking at him. In his early thirties, he'd filled out a bit, growing into his tall frame and square jaw, never losing that boyish grin that had won her over from the first glance.

"Dodging the rain?" he asked, motioning to the window, where sure enough, the panes were splattered.

"Just work..." She wondered now how long she'd been sitting here, trying to move forward, when instead, she was just slipping backward, thinking about her days in that bakery instead of the promotion she'd been working toward for years.

"On a Sunday?" He gave her a look of mock disapproval.

"I can't exactly let my day job fall by the wayside while I'm at the bakery," she reminded him. "I'm working on an article. It's...why I'm in town."

"Something about Hope Hollow?" His interest seemed to have been piqued.

"More like the experience of owning a small business." She shrugged. "It's not going well but I have time."

"Your grandmother said you're a journalist." Then, looking a little pink in the cheeks himself, elaborated: "She likes to brag about you."

Carly laughed to cover the flutter she felt that he'd inquired about her. Or at least, gleaned some news about her.

But then she thought about how her grandmother had always liked Nick. How she'd been just as surprised and disappointed when things ended as Carly was.

How it was awfully strange that Nana hadn't mentioned Nick yet. But then, since Carly hadn't either, she probably assumed Carly didn't know yet and didn't want to give her a reason to leave town early.

Her grandmother was waiting for them to run into each other. Like they had. A few times now.

"She would," Carly said, thinking of how Nana would often stand at the counter in the bakery, boasting about her granddaughters' accomplishments to the customers. "But I'm not a journalist. I work for a lifestyle magazine and this article might not even get published. I pull research, proofread, that sort of thing. It's far from glamorous." Or exciting. Or fulfilling.

Or...meaningful. Whereas what Nana did was much more than stir up a perfect cake batter. She brought a smile to people's faces. When they came to pick it up, and later, when they ate it.

"Not to hear Nana Parker tell it." Nick tipped his head. "So...you like it?"

"My job?" She blinked a few times, unsure how to even answer that question. Once there had been a time she liked it, or at least, thought she would. "It pays the bills," she managed to say. *For now*, she added to herself. And even then, just barely.

"Well, there must be something about it that you like if it's keeping you there," Nick said.

Carly opened her mouth to agree but found that she couldn't, not really. "It's just a job. Maybe there's a chance for it to be something more, but..." But that was becoming increasingly unlikely.

"Well, then someone perhaps?"

Carly raised her eyebrows, deciding there wasn't anything to hide. No pretense to keep up. No ego to maintain. They hadn't parted on those conditions. They'd cared about each other, even loved each other. But that was years ago. And like him, she'd moved on. At least, that's what he thought. Maybe even what she thought, until coming back here proved otherwise.

She looked across the table at the only boy she'd ever loved, now a man, a father. The years had been good to him, but there must have been tough times too. A sadness of how much she didn't know about him settled into the silence.

"Friends, sure," she said. Friends to go out for drinks with on Friday nights, or maybe join for a yoga class on Sundays. But her closest friend remained Joanna, who faithfully visited every few months, and called much more often than that. Who knew her inside and out. Her history. Her heart.

And who also hadn't tipped her off about Nick being back in Hope Hollow.

"Most of the people I know are from work. It's where I

spend most of my time." Carly knew that was a gross understatement. The hours were long, and more and more, she felt like she was on a hamster wheel, doing the same thing day after day and never getting anywhere.

He gave a nod, but she thought she saw something pass through his dark gaze. "I never figured you for one who'd stay away. You always talked about coming back here after college."

"Yes, well, I was young then. I didn't know what I wanted yet."

And looking at Nick, she still wasn't sure. His eyes met hers and her stomach went a little funny, fighting off the attraction that had survived the worst kind of heartbreak. For a long time, she'd feared this exact moment. Sitting across from him. Talking to him. Pretending that what they'd once had never existed.

It was enough to keep her away, that and all the other memories that only lived on in this town.

But now, she saw that Nick held a piece of her past. Much like Hope Hollow. An entire part of her life that she would struggle to part with again, knowing now that when she ever did return, some parts of her wouldn't even be around to remember.

She was about to ask about his surprising career path when Nick glanced at his watch.

"Well, I should probably pick up Daisy. She's at a crafts class next door, and if I'm late, she tends to worry."

"That's sweet," Carly said, grinning.

"For now. But I'm not sure if I'll like her fretting over me when she's a teenager," he said with a laugh which was swiftly met with a loud "shh" and a glare from the silver-haired librarian.

Nick raised his eyebrows at Carly and she covered her mouth to smother her own laughter.

"Some things never change in this town," she whispered, recalling that the very same librarian had once given her and Joanna the boot for giggling too hard one snowy afternoon.

Nick's smile turned fond. "And isn't that wonderful?"

Their gazes locked for a beat and Carly pulled back in her chair, starting to clear her throat and then thinking the better of it when she caught the librarian's stern stare.

"So your daughter watches out for you then?" she asked, getting back to their conversation.

Nick gave a weary nod. "I think she's picking it up from my mother, who seems to think that I need a hot meal provided for me whenever I'm not at the station."

"I seem to recall your mother being an excellent cook," she pointed out, her smile turning wistful. "I remember struggling to concentrate on the music notes when she had a soup simmering on the stove in the kitchen."

Nick laughed, a sound that she hadn't heard in so long but still had the ability to make her stomach flutter after all this time, and this time the librarian all but hissed in their direction. Nick ignored it, saying, "I seem to recall you sticking around a little bit after your lesson."

"Guilty as charged," she said, raising her hand. Only not just for the food. She'd stayed for Nick. For more time to be with him, even if he didn't know it.

The table fell silent, and she felt like they'd turned back time, to when she was still a nervous teenager trying to get her footing, to know where she stood. Nick wasn't married anymore. And he was back in Hope Hollow.

And she was just passing through, she reminded herself firmly.

Nick must have seen the way she was staring at her laptop because he tapped the table and said, "Well, I'll leave you to it."

"Maybe I'll see Daisy one day at the bakery this week?" Carly asked.

But what she really meant was that she hoped she would see him there too.

Nick stood and looked at her for a long moment. "I'm sure you will," he said, before walking away.

six

On Monday morning, after they'd made three-dozen muffins, two pies, prepped the batter for three-dozen brownies, and filled the display case with the usual morning offerings, Jill announced that she had a business meeting later in the day.

Carly had been stifling a yawn when Jill suddenly spoke. Up until now, the three had worked in quiet companionship in the kitchen. Now, gripping the mug that held her third cup of coffee, Carly glanced at Becca, who was frowning at their older sister.

"What kind of a meeting?" she asked slowly. "You mean with the buyers?"

"*Prospective* buyers, right?" Carly corrected. Now two sets of eyes flashed on her and then her sisters went back to their conversation. It was a topic they were both familiar with, picking up wherever they'd left off before her return, but Carly couldn't fight back the temper that was stirring.

She set down her coffee. "This *is* a family business. Don't I have a say?"

Now Jill looked at her. Her eyes were round, whether insulted or angry, Carly couldn't be sure, and she folded her arms over her chest. "A say? Carly, you have a career that has nothing to do with this bakery. You left town ten years ago and never looked back."

Carly should have known this would come up eventually, and it looked like the time was now. Jill had been vocal ten years ago about Carly's decision to go away to college instead of somewhere local. And Jill's thoughts on her decision to stay in Philadelphia had never gone unnoticed, even if they weren't often shared anymore.

"That's not true." Carly's voice was small with hurt, but also because her sister's words were partly true. "I haven't been to town, but it doesn't mean I stopped caring." She hesitated, wondering if now would be a good time to mention the article. If Jill might see it as a chance to put their little bakery on the map, and drive a little traffic from surrounding areas that hadn't given it a chance before.

But one look at Jill's stony gaze told her otherwise.

"I'm still a part of this family, and this bakery is as much a part of my childhood as our house. If you were planning to sell that, I'd speak up," Carly pointed out.

"It's Nana's house," Jill corrected.

Carly tipped her head, exasperated. "You know what I mean. We grew up in that house. And in this bakery."

Jill pressed her lips tighter as if stifling a sigh. "Okay, then. What do you want to say?"

"What if there was another way?" Carly asked, even though she didn't have any ideas.

"There isn't another way," Jill said flatly.

"We've really tried everything," Becca added, her tone gentle if resigned. "But if you can think of something else..." She looked so hopeful that for a minute Carly wondered if she should tell them about the article, but one glance at Jill's set jaw told her otherwise.

She didn't need Jill telling her not to write the article. Didn't need Jill making her job more difficult than it already was. How was she supposed to get to the heart of the story when the soul had come out of this place?

"I'm here now. I'm helping." She decided not to bother offering any random thoughts for the place. In the mood Jill was in right now, chances were high that she wouldn't be open to any new ideas.

"And soon you'll be gone." Jill tossed up her hands and pushed back into the kitchen, the door swinging in her wake.

"Let her go," Becca said, holding Carly back by the arm.

"How is this so easy for her?" Carly accused. She lifted her mug to sip her coffee, but even that did little to lift her spirits.

"Oh, this is far from easy for any of us." Becca gave an unhappy laugh and straightened the already perfectly placed baskets that filled the bakery case. "And I know it doesn't look like it, but Jill's taking it the hardest. That's why she's so upset today. Just the thought of having this meeting makes it feel real to her. Makes her...afraid, I think."

"Of change? Or losing the bakery?"

"Both? She's spent more time here than either of us ever

did. And she doesn't have anything else to fall back on. I was...almost married." Here Becca paused. "And you have your job in Philly. And Jill doesn't have much going on outside of these four walls. Between the two of us, I think she's scared."

"Then why do it? Why sell?"

"Because there's no other option. People were coming here for Nana more than her sweets. We're still making her recipes, but somehow it's just not the same coming from us. We're overworked and broke and we've run out of ideas for keeping the bakery going. If you find one, tell us, but we've probably already considered it."

"What about expanding the services?"

"Expanding?" Becca's eyes grew wide and then, to Carly's disappointment, she started to laugh. "But how? We're already spread thin; we never get a break. We've sacrificed everything for this place."

Even though Carly knew that Becca wasn't blaming her outright for her engagement ending when Jonah moved away, she couldn't fight the guilt that she hadn't been here, helping out, when she was needed the most.

And worse, no one in her family had thought to ask for her.

"But what will you do, Becca?" she asked gently, wondering if she was ready to hear the truth. That her sisters had new plans. That they were ready to say goodbye to this bakery and all the memories that had been made here.

Just like she'd done ten years ago.

But Becca just shook her head. "I don't know what I'll

do yet. We'd get money from the sale. It would give us some options. Maybe I'll go into catering. Or try something new."

"You love to bake," Carly said. Jonah had claimed that Becca loved it more than him. That she'd chosen her past over their future. These four walls over a house they might have shared together.

After losing her relationship to stay and run the bakery, how could she shutter the doors now?

Becca raised an eyebrow. "Not as much as Jill. But probably more than you."

Carly frowned and reached for her coffee again. "I like to bake. I just…"

"Don't love it," Becca finished for her.

Carly blinked a few times. Was that what her sisters thought? And was it even true? She didn't even know anymore. For so many years, this bakery, this kitchen, these recipes, were her life—one that she didn't question. But this bakery was full of more than flour and sugar and cakes and cookies. It was full of memories. Good and bad. And eventually, the bad won out. When she'd moved out of Hope Hollow, she'd tried to put it all behind her, even succeeded for a while there.

Just like she'd managed to do with Nick.

But she'd loved him.

And she loved this bakery.

And being back in town, having it all back…she wasn't sure she could leave again knowing that if she ever returned it would all be gone.

"Let me at least try to help. Please. I…might have a way."

Becca didn't give an answer, but Carly took that as a good sign.

It gave her reason to hope. At least a little bit.

The prospective buyers came in after the lunch rush. Middle-aged men in suits, looking as out of place in Hope Hollow as Carly felt half the time. They carried leather-bound folders, and financial papers were spread out over the back table where Jill sat hunched with them for close to an hour.

After watching the interaction from behind the counter and hearing nothing, Carly decided that some small-town hospitality was in order. She knew all too well how much her coworkers relied on their daily corporate coffee. Their factory-made Danishes, all cut the same size and guaranteed to taste the same day after day, month after month.

People here in Hope Hollow would probably like whatever this franchise had to offer too, admittedly. But Carly didn't like it one bit.

She cut three thick slices of Nana's famous strawberry pie and walked over to the table, watching as Jill's eyes grew as she approached. She flicked a nervous glance to the gentlemen and then back to Carly as if trying to silently communicate with her eyes to go away.

Carly put on her sweetest smile and put one foot in front of the other.

"Can I offer you all some homemade strawberry pie?" She didn't wait for an answer when she set the plates down on top of their spreadsheets, her lips pinching at the corporate logo stamped in the top left corner of each page.

"This is my youngest sister, Carly," Jill explained a little breathlessly. To Carly, her eyes flashed as she accepted her plate.

"A pleasure to meet you," the older man said, extending his hand.

Carly gave both of them a firm handshake, showing she wasn't here just to deliver pie. She saw the younger man wince a little at her grip.

"Homemade strawberry pie. A secret family recipe," Carly told them.

"Don't mind if I do." The younger guy had composed himself and now seemed to perk up as he lifted his fork to his mouth. "Wow, this is good."

The older man chewed thoughtfully. "Strawberry pie. No rhubarb?"

"Just strawberry," Carly said with a smile that she certainly didn't feel. "One of our bestselling items here at Sunrise. There's nothing like homemade pie, is there? Baked with love, isn't that what Nana always said, Jill?"

Jill's mouth was pinched. She didn't touch her slice of pie, but then, she already knew what it tasted like, and she knew it was better than anything these two suits could offer.

"Well, enjoy," Carly said, and finally walked off, leaving the men to eat their pie and Jill to fume.

She busied herself at the counter, taking down a birthday cake order for a woman who was surprising her husband for his fiftieth, but even as she wrote up the details, she kept an eye on the table. Jill was looking at the paperwork now. Carly could see the hesitation on her face as she reviewed it. One man was offering her a pen. A pen!

Carly's heart hammered while she waited to see if her sister would take it. Her shoulders finally sagged when she saw Jill shake her head.

"Carly."

Carly jumped when Becca scooted past her, tsking under her breath. "We have customers at the bakery case," she whispered. "Didn't you see?"

Carly shook away her carelessness. "Sorry, Bec. I...was distracted."

Becca gave her a teasing frown and went to help Erika and her two little boys, who were pressing their palms against the glass case, leaving fingerprints behind.

Carly decided to make a fresh pot of coffee, but when she saw Jill push her chair back and stand, she decided to head to the kitchen instead.

So much for that. Jill wasted no time in speed walking across the bakery, her smile tight while the men still hovered near the door, no doubt taking in the space once again, imagining where their standard counter and tables would fit.

"What was that all about?" Jill whispered, following her into the kitchen.

"What was what about?" Carly asked innocently. She took a clean mixing bowl from the shelf and then moved to the fridge for some eggs. "I just wanted to make the gentlemen feel welcome. Couldn't send them on their way hungry. Where are they driving in from? Boston? New York?"

Jill's mouth thinned but she didn't say anything more.

Instead, she walked back out through the swinging door and came through it again, carrying three baskets of the remaining muffins, followed by Becca. Jill's eyes looked tired when she began consolidating the muffins.

"We beat the rush. Why don't you take a break?" Becca suggested.

"The day's almost over," Jill said, shaking her head.

Becca brushed some crumbs from the counter. "Then let me do the leftovers run tonight. I insist."

Jill nodded slowly. "That will give me more time to prep for tomorrow." She walked over to the bulletin board where they always posted tomorrow's specials and then heaved out a sigh that Carly could see roll through her shoulders. "Turnovers tomorrow." Meaning puff pastry.

It had always been one of Carly's favorite things to do as a child, the rolling and chilling, the way, if done properly—which was a must here at Sunrise—the end result would be flaky and buttery.

"You guys go on," Carly offered. "I'll prep for tomorrow!"

Jill looked doubtful. "It's a lot of work."

"I'm aware of that!" Carly smiled to show that she had it covered, even though she hadn't closed up the bakery in years. But how difficult could it be? Like riding a bike, surely. Or at least, like whipping up her grandmother's lemon squares.

"You sure?" Becca looked just as eager to leave as she was to stay, and Carly could only shake her head.

"I'll be fine. And if I have a question, I know where to find you."

"I had hoped to do some laundry tonight," Becca admitted. "And my favorite show is on, too."

"That's more like it. I'm not sending you home early just to do housework. You guys deserve a night off, for some fun." Sensing their resistance, she added, "You may as well take advantage of me being here, right?"

"I suppose it would be nice to tend to my garden before the sun sets." Jill was always an avid gardener, following in their mother's footsteps and using herbs in the bread she baked each morning. She still lived in the small cottage near the center of town that she'd moved into in her early twenties.

"Then it's settled." Carly shooed her sisters out of the back door like a mother duck encouraging her ducklings across the street. They went reluctantly, especially Jill, and when Carly finally closed the door behind them and leaned against it, she wondered for a moment just what she had done.

Once the stragglers had left for the day and she turned the sign on the storefront, Carly wiped down the tables and counter. Then she went to the kitchen, deciding that if she was going to be here for a while, she may as well make herself something to eat.

The recipes they used in the bakery were mostly memorized, some posted on the bulletin board, along with notes about inventory orders, supplies they needed, and ideas for seasonal items. Carly studied it now, but her gaze drifted to the framed photograph that hung beside it, one of the sisters when they were much younger. Carly must have only been about three in the photo, with pigtails and full cheeks, a mouth stained with chocolate, and a wooden spoon in her hand. Jill was protectively holding the batter as if trying to make sure Carly wouldn't steal anymore, and Becca was wedged between them, her smile radiant.

The Sunrise Sisters. That's what they'd been back then, and not just because of the name of this bakery. They were happy. Life was simple. Their futures were spread out before them, even if it was already planned, assumed from their birth that they'd take over the family business, and pass it down to the next generation of women.

Carly's heart sank a little when she thought of how it had all turned out.

"Nothing something sweet can't fix," she said to herself. In the small office off the supply closet that housed an ancient wooden desk, piles of invoices, and, she realized with dismay, unpaid bills, was where the family's recipe binder was kept. Under lock and key. None of the secret recipes were in there. No, Nana claimed those were kept in her head only, but Carly suspected long ago that they were jotted down somewhere, not that she was yet to find them.

She pressed the numbers into the safe (her mother's birthday; hadn't changed) and removed the binder, she couldn't help but smile when she saw the familiar handwriting. Recipes tweaked over the years, evidenced by little notes in a different ink color. Sometimes a photo tossed in, or a note.

"Carly loved it!" said a note beside the turtle pie.

Carly smiled, knowing that she was seven when she'd first tried it and loved the name, though the taste was nothing to ignore either.

"Jill's birthday cake!" was scribbled next to a recipe for strawberry cake, complete with pink frosting.

And there, tucked at the end of the recipe book, was a photo that stole her breath for a second, even though she'd stared at it hundreds of times before. It was taken the same day as the photo of her and her sisters, only in this one, their mother and Nana stood proudly behind them. And in this one, Jill wasn't wrestling the mixing bowl from Carly's hands. No, in this one, Carly was holding her mother's hand.

Her eyes drifted now into the kitchen, to the counter, where the photo was set. She closed her eyes against the image of her mother standing there, laughing at something as she mixed dough.

Carly slammed the book closed and put it back in its place.

Tonight, she'd keep it simple. Her stomach rumbled as she walked back into the kitchen and made a list of what she'd need to do before she turned out the lights. The space was mostly cleaned, the storefront closed up, and even though Jill had left a list of everything they'd be baking in the morning, the menu was the same as it always was.

Once, it was what brought people back day after day.

Carly tackled most of the prep work, mixing dough that would need to chill, washing up, careful not to leave any mess, and then, to treat herself, decided to whip up a simple cookie batter. By the time they finished baking, she'd have made her way through much of the list. By the time she finished eating them, she'd be ready to head home.

Fetching an extra mixing bowl and cookie sheet, she measured out the ingredients and stirred the batter, her stomach rumbling the entire time. The oven was preheated by the time she had scooped out twelve perfect mounds, and she could bring the remaining cookies to Nana, who never could pass up a cookie, even if she never finished one.

The cookies went into the oven on the middle rack and Carly quickly washed up the evidence of her work. She scanned the list, crossing off items just to be sure that she hadn't missed anything. Just to prove to Jill how invested she was in this place, she even bundled up the trash bags and carried them to the dumpster behind the building.

Jill couldn't argue that she was getting a lot done. So much that she'd lost track of time.

She frowned at that realization. She hadn't set the egg timer, only the timer on the stove. Now, walking back into the kitchen, her nose started to twitch at a smell that was very unfamiliar in this kitchen—something was burning.

The timer had never gone off.

Oh no. No! She'd forgotten what Becca had said about the oven—how they were down to two and that one needed to be serviced.

Smoke billowed out and she hurried to the back door, but it was a warm night, not a breeze to be found, and the smoke kept coming.

The alarm blared, the sound almost a worse sensation than the smoke that was making her cough. She grabbed a stool, stood up, and pushed at the device with one hand while attempting to cover her ears (or ear) with the other. It stopped only to start again.

Jill was going to be furious when she found out, and Becca too. They'd probably kick her out, and never let her back. That was if she didn't burn the place down before they had a chance to sell.

Grabbing an oven mitt, she slid it on and yanked open the door to the oven, pulling the burnt cookies from the oven and dropping them onto the island with a crash. The door to the back alley was still cracked and she opened it wider, sighing heavily with relief.

There. The kitchen would air out, even if it took all night. By the morning, she could have this place looking like new. Her sisters would be none the wiser.

The sound of sirens made her stop for a moment. She blinked, then looked through the window of the kitchen door and into the storefront, where a firetruck was pulling up through the big, paned window.

Fat chance of Jill never finding out.

But that was the least of Carly's problems because as she walked into the storefront, trying her best to regain a shred of her dignity, she came face to face through the glass window with Nick Sutton, illuminated by the flashing lights of a firetruck.

SEVEN

For a minute there, Nick wasn't sure that Carly was going to unlock the door and let him inside. Her gaze flicked from him to the kitchen door enough times for him to wonder if there was a false alarm. But finally, after what looked like a very large sigh on her part, one that rolled through her shoulders, Carly reached up and turned the lock.

"We got a call from the alarm company." He looked over Carly's shoulders for any sign of fire, but he was guessing by her lack of urgency that whatever happened was under control by now.

"We have an alarm system?" She blinked up at him with those big eyes that made his gut tighten the way it used to every time he picked her up here on a hot summer afternoon, both of them eager to get to the lake, and not just to swim.

He checked himself quickly. He was on duty. And Carly was off limits.

"It was Jill's idea. She had it installed a few years ago.

Good idea, if you ask me." Nick stepped farther into the storefront, then motioned to his partner that he would take it from here.

"Fire's out?" He started making his way back to the kitchen with long, even strides, but Carly remained in place near the door.

"Well, there's no fire," Carly said. "I just…"

She mumbled something under her breath, something he couldn't hear. He stepped closer to her instead, craning his neck. "What was that?"

"I…was…making cookies."

He cocked an eyebrow, doing his best to fight off a smile. "You burned the cookies?"

"It wasn't like that!" Carly protested as a flush rose in her cheeks. "It was the oven timer!"

He shook his head. "More like you're out of practice."

"Stop!" She glared at him but it was a little hard to take her seriously when she had soot on her cheek and the tip of her nose and her hair looked like it had been yanked from its ponytail in some sort of frenzy.

"Well, I do need to check everything out. Policy."

She nodded miserably, then held out a hand toward the kitchen door, leading the way.

He stepped inside the kitchen to see dark balls of what might have been cookies turned out on the workbench. The back door was open and a cool breeze filtered in, diffusing the smell of smoke.

He looked inside the oven with the open door. "This one the culprit?"

Now Carly was struggling to fight a smile. "Stop. It's broken. Becca told me but I forgot."

"You shouldn't be using it," he said. "I could tape it off for you?"

Now Carly blanched. "You're not serious."

He laughed lightly. "No. But I could." He picked up one of the cookies. The thing could have been used for a hockey puck in his winter bar league.

"Don't judge," she warned him, folding her arms across her chest. "I'm not out of practice, either. I bake all the time in my apartment. I'm just not used to this kitchen."

"Well, I could lecture you on being more careful, but I'll save the speech." He grinned at her, but she wasn't amused.

"I would appreciate it if you wouldn't mention any of this to my sisters."

He winced. "No can do."

"Let me guess. Policy?"

"Jill and Becca are the legal owners. Unless your name is—"

"It's not." She sighed. "My grandmother must have officially signed it over to them when she retired. Maybe she needed to do that for..."

He frowned at her. "For what? Seems like a formality to me, not sure why she even bothered with the paperwork."

Carly opened her mouth like she wanted to say something and then stopped herself.

"I guess I should start packing my bags then. Jill won't let me step foot in this place again once she hears what happened."

"Don't do that," he said, only realizing how that had

come across when her eyes snapped up to his. They stared at each other for a moment, until he was all too aware that they were alone in this kitchen, the air was still heavy with smoke, and she was a girl that he'd hurt. Badly.

She probably couldn't wait to be rid of him.

But he wasn't ready to let go of her. Not again.

"You have a little..." He held up a hand, and Carly looked at him with wide eyes. She brought a hand to her face, then rubbed it, but she only managed to smudge the soot, spreading it farther over her face.

"Here." He pulled some paper towels from the roll and ran them under the tap. Gently, carefully, he brushed it over her cheek, taking his time, feeling something shift in his groin when their eyes met.

He cleared his throat. "You have some on your nose too."

Now she gave him a mischievous smile. "Something tells me that you were considering not mentioning that for a while."

He grinned, relaxing into the mood, remembering how easy it had always been to talk to her. He hadn't felt this way in a long time. Not since he'd been back to Hope Hollow.

Not for many years before that.

"Let me stay and help you clean up." There wasn't much to do other than get rid of the burned cookies and scrub the baking sheet—or, knowing Carly, bury it deep in the dumpster where Jill would never find it.

"You don't need to get back to the station?" Carly asked. "What if there's an emergency?"

He shrugged. "My shift's over. I was actually heading out

when the call came through. When I saw it was the bakery... Well, this place is special."

She pursed her lips. "Wish more people thought so."

He looked at her sharply. "What's that supposed to mean?"

"Nothing." She shook her head and pulled a trash bag from a lower cabinet, dumping the cookies and—sure enough—the pan into it. "I'm just tired. And hungry."

"I could go for a pizza right about now if you feel like sharing one." His pulse skipped a beat when he realized what he was suggesting. He hadn't thought through how she might react, or if he was overstepping. He just knew that he'd missed her, thought about her more than he ever should have, and that now she was standing here, soot in her hair, a frown on her pretty mouth, somehow she'd never looked more beautiful.

"Unless you have to get back to your grandmother. Or your sisters," he said, giving her a graceful exit. No need to make things awkward. They both knew why things had ended. They both understood. It wasn't about not caring about each other.

And he'd never stopped caring about her. The question was, had she stopped caring about him?

It would be selfish to have expected her not to, especially when he'd moved on, at least physically. Had a family of his own, a career, and a life in Boston. For a little while at least.

She gave him a sidelong glance. "You want to get a pizza together?"

His pulse skipped again. She hadn't said no, and for some reason, that thrilled him more than it probably should.

"Hey, I have to eat, too. And I'm going to work up an appetite getting this place in order."

"What about..."

He knew what she was going to ask. "Daisy's with my parents tonight. When I have a later shift, my mom stays over. I think she likes the excuse to be out of the house, honestly. She's there alone so much since my dad's still putting in long hours at the hospital."

Carly hesitated again while Nick held his breath, telling himself that if she declined, he'd be no worse off than he'd been a week ago before she'd come back to town.

But instead, she gave a little shrug and said, "I can't think of a reason to say no."

He grinned. Neither could he.

If Maria Concetti had any opinions about Nick holding the door open for Carly to pass, the woman managed to keep them to herself.

But from the gleam in her eyes when she seated them in the corner and then all but sprinted back to the kitchen, Carly was fairly sure that the phone chain had started and that by morning, everyone would be talking about Carly and Nick and speculating just what had led to this event.

So long as the part about the firetruck pulling up to the bakery wasn't mentioned as well, then she could live with it.

"Our usual?" Nick asked after taking a cursory glance at the menu and setting it down.

She swallowed back her surprise, needing a moment to

recover from the fact that Nick still remembered what they used to order here. Did that mean he thought of their time together as often as she did? It dwindled over the years, of course, as she'd hoped it would, but every once in a while, she saw something that reminded her of him. A checkered tablecloth like the one beneath her fingertips right now. A song on the radio that he always liked to crank up and sing along to on their drives out to the lake.

"I could probably do with some wine, too." She added quickly, "I mean, after nearly burning down the bakery."

In other words, not because this was anything romantic. Even if a part of her wished that it was.

But they needn't have asked. A few minutes later, Maria returned to their table with two glasses and a bottle of red wine, giving a little wink when she set it down on the table.

"On the house," she said, and then, lifting her chin before they could even protest, said, "On the house or no food. That's the deal."

Nick laughed while he poured the wine. Oh, that sound again! No matter how long the day, he always managed to pull a smile from her face and put her in the best mood.

He still did, she realized. She reached for her glass, taking a sip, hoping that it meant that they wouldn't have to endure an awkward toast, because what would they even toast to? Being back in town? Because she wasn't. Not really. She was just visiting. And it was worse than she'd ever feared it would be.

Better too.

"In that case, we'll take the house special and tiramisu for dessert," Nick said.

"Of course, the only dessert I would dare to make. Nothing compares to Nana Parker," Maria said with a smile as she collected their menus.

"Isn't that the truth?" Nick said to Carly.

Carly nodded wearily. "It would appear so. I don't think business has been the same since she retired."

Nick frowned at her. "Is everything okay with the business? I've...heard some rumors."

"Rumors?" She stared at him, feeling the reality of the situation heavy on her shoulders. If word was already spreading through town, then it must really be happening. But how could people let it? And which place would be next? Concetti's?

She bit back a smile, thinking that Maria would stick Frankie on a prospective buyer sooner than she'd shutter this place.

"Talk around town," Nick clarified. "I don't think anyone ever expected your grandmother to retire."

"Me included," Carly said, sighing. "Her arthritis was always bad, but I hadn't realized how much it was affecting her."

Carly hesitated, unsure how much she could tell him without betraying her family but then decided that they didn't have much left to lose. "Honestly, I'm not sure what's going to happen to the bakery. But...sales are down, and the place needs some work. The bakery's been a beloved part of this community for years. Maybe people just need time to adjust to Nana's absence."

"She certainly made it special," Nick said with a smile

that tugged straight at her heart. "How's she doing? Not being there every day must be an adjustment."

Carly thought about the hole in Nana's hedge and laughed. "I think she's going a little stir-crazy. But she keeps busy."

"Having you home must help," he offered.

There wasn't much to say to that. Nothing that didn't stir up feelings of guilt and regret. And worry.

"Try telling my sisters that," she joked instead. "I think they're still mad at me for moving away. At least Jill is."

Nick gave her a look of understanding, reminding her that he knew all about her family dynamic, even been witness to a few of the sisterly conflicts.

"So, you miss your city life yet?"

Carly hesitated, torn between making her life out to be better than it was and bonding with Nick the way they used to do. He'd been so easy to talk to, to share her problems with as well as her dreams.

"Yes and no," she finally said. "My job keeps me busy but it hasn't been as satisfying as I'd hoped. I've kept going, waiting for it to turn into something bigger. I'm almost there..." But without a killer article, she wasn't going to get her boss's attention. She looked at Nick, unsure if she wanted to even ask him the same. "How about you? Have you adjusted to being back in Hope Hollow?"

"Yes and no." He grinned at his word choice and his deep brown eyes crinkled at the corners. "It's certainly a different pace of life, and it's a good place for kids. Daisy seems happy." Now he frowned a little.

"And your job?" she asked. "I don't remember you ever talking about becoming a firefighter." But then, she'd only really known him for a small time, ten years ago. She couldn't expect him to have the same dreams and desires as he did back then.

She certainly hadn't followed the path she'd intended.

He looked up at her. "I was in management consulting back in Boston. I liked it. A lot, actually." His eyes turned wistful for one telling second and then he shrugged. "But it was long hours, two working parents, and Daisy...it didn't seem fair to Daisy. When I moved back, I didn't see much room for consulting here in town, and the fire station has been like a second home. A family in a way. Daisy needed that. I did too."

Maria interrupted them to set a pizza tray on the center of the table, giving a less than subtle look in Nick's direction before she walked away.

"It's a good thing we're talking business or I'd say she was getting ideas about us," Carly whispered to him.

"Oh, she's had ideas from the moment the door opened," Nick replied with a grin. If this bothered him, he didn't let on, and neither did she.

The town would talk, of course. Probably Nana had already received a call from Maria. More than probably. Certainly. When Carly looked over at the counter, she saw Maria try to crouch down and then, perhaps realizing that she'd been caught and that any action would make it even more obvious, she gave a little sniff and started folding napkins.

Carly could only smile.

"What's so funny?" Nick asked.

"Just...being back here. It's nice. Even if half the town is probably aware of what we're doing right now."

Nick laughed. He lifted the wine bottle and refilled their glasses. "I've learned not to let things like that bother me. People think what they will, especially in a town this small. I'm sure they've said a lot about me since I've been back."

Carly thought about what Becca had told her, wondering if her sisters even had the facts right.

"And what do they say?" she asked, reaching for her glass.

"Probably that I don't get out enough," he said with a shrug. Then he lifted his glass. "To getting me out of the house."

Was that all it took? Coming back to town to reunite with her first true love? Her only true love?

Even she knew that it wasn't that easy. Not for her. Not for anyone.

"I bet there are plenty of women in town who would be happy to keep you company," she said, glancing at him.

He shrugged again. "Maybe so, but if there is anything I've learned, it's that it's better to be alone than with the wrong person."

And tonight, he wasn't choosing to be alone.

She lifted her glass and tapped it to his. Relief that she had no business feeling made her relax in her chair while Nick served her a slice of pizza, so hot that the cheese stretched off the knife.

"Oh." She groaned after the first bite, then shook her head. "I forgot how good the sauce is. There's something so authentic about a family recipe."

"*Secret* family recipe!" Maria called out from across the room, before disappearing back into the kitchen.

"You Parkers have plenty of secret recipes from what I recall," Nick teased.

"Yes, but for some reason, people only seem to want them if they're baked by Nana herself."

Carly's frustration must have been obvious because Nick hesitated and then said, "I could help. I mean, offer suggestions. If you want. I don't want to overstep, but this is the sort of thing I used to do. Come in, look at what worked, and what didn't. That sort of thing."

"Seriously? You'd do that?" Carly stared at him across the table, the pizza almost forgotten as newfound hope built in her chest.

"Of course," he said good-naturedly.

"I'd have to ask my sister..." Carly grimaced, just thinking about Jill's defeated attitude lately. But then she thought about what Becca had said. About how Jill wanted the bakery to thrive more than the rest of them. "You let me worry about Jill."

"And you let me worry about the bakery," Nick said. "Between the two of us, I'm sure we'll figure something out."

Between the two of them. It made her feel like they shared something, not just a past with a sad ending. But as for the future, it had never been more unclear.

eight

After checking her phone compulsively the entire walk to the bakery, Carly braced herself when she approached the kitchen the next morning. No messages from Jill. No warnings from Becca. Maybe she wasn't walking into an ambush after all.

Her insides felt like jelly when she pulled the door from the back lot, which was only partly due to the fear of her sister's wrath and somewhat the result of an evening spent in Nick's company.

She'd replayed the events over and over again as she'd lay in bed, staring at the ceiling, just like she'd done ten years ago, after their first date at the very pizza parlor they'd gone to last night. Sure, it was the only pizza parlor in Hope Hollow, but she couldn't help feeling like they'd come full circle.

"I saw you used the third oven last night," Jill said as Carly wrapped an apron around her waist. "That's the one with no temperature control, and the timer doesn't work either."

"Sorry." Carly gulped. Should she confess now? Was Nick waiting until he knew Jill was in the bakery to tell her what had happened?

There was no room for hypothetical scenarios, she told herself. She and Nick had shared a nice evening. But what more could happen beyond that? And it was hardly a reason to spare her feelings. Especially when he was a professional and there were procedures to follow.

"You could have burned the entire place down!" Jill shook her head as she poured the coffee cake batter into a Bundt tin.

Carly pulled a mixing bowl from the shelf and decided to come out with it. She was almost thirty, and the worst her sister could do was kick her out of the bakery, but she didn't think that Jill would.

Jill's name might be on the business papers, but this was a family bakery. She couldn't get rid of Carly that easily. Maybe once, when Carly was younger and feeling excluded became a good reason to shorten her hours and spend that time pursuing other interests. Other people. But this bakery wouldn't succeed without all of their input now, including hers. And she suspected that Jill knew that too. Even if she hadn't said as much.

"Not with that fancy alarm system you have," Carly replied with a little smile. "It goes off at the first whiff of smoke."

Now Jill looked up at her sharply. "It didn't!" Then, realizing that Carly wasn't joking: "Did the firetruck pull up?"

Becca looked at Carly with wide eyes. It was hard to tell if she was scared or curious. Probably a mixture of both.

"Of course it did. And before you ask, yes, Nick was on duty."

"Oh my!" Becca's lips curved into a smile, but she quickly sobered her expression when she realized that Jill wasn't so amused.

Jill set the spatula in the mixing bowl and fixed Carly with a stare. "You were supposed to be prepping!"

"I did! But then I got hungry," Carly said, suddenly feeling like she was five years old again and she'd been caught eating too much raw cookie dough, cutting into the batch they'd promised for the ladies' luncheon down at the gardening club.

"But there wasn't a fire..." Ah, Becca. Always the peacemaker.

"Just smoke. And that's all it took to trigger the taxpayers' resources, so...you might want to think about that," Carly said to Jill.

That officially silenced her oldest sister, but the tension remained while they worked. As much as Carly was eager to tell them both about Nick's offer to help with the bakery, now was probably not the best time.

"I can do the turnovers if you want," she said instead. A peace offering, she hoped. "You know how much I like to make puff pastry."

Jill looked like she wanted to decline, but only Nana could be that stubborn. Pastry was time-consuming, and it would free up Jill to start on their other usual items. The tried and true recipes that had been in their family for generations, just like the pizza and pasta at Concetti's.

Only people didn't seem to be popping in for those baked goods as much anymore. Could it really be because Nana wasn't here to serve them? Carly suspected there was more to this and that maybe Nick *would* be able to get to the bottom of it.

"What if we added raisins? Or cranberries?" Carly said, already reaching for the flour to start the dough.

The kitchen fell silent and Becca's hands stilled as she looked in horror at Jill. Jill blinked several times before saying evenly, "The recipe doesn't call for raisins or cranberries."

"But people might like something different," Carly said, not to be deterred.

She waited for it, and it came. The glance between her two older sisters. The silent communication that always seemed to leave her out, the third wheel, the rebel, the one who once ate all the cookie dough, and now, dared to suggest something new.

Becca went back to scooping out scones and Jill just shook her head. "Just follow the recipe, please. That's what works."

Except, Carly thought to herself, that maybe it didn't work anymore.

The afternoon crowd was thin, and the bakery case was still half-filled by three. Whoever was scheduled to get the leftovers tonight would be pleased, Carly thought, as she looked up when the bells over the door jangled.

She was happy to see Daisy approaching the counter.

"Hello, Daisy! It's nice to see you again. Will it be your usual today?" she asked, remembering the child's preference.

The little girl grinned. "Yes, please!"

Carly had set aside an oatmeal cookie just in case Daisy stopped by today.

"I won't be here for long, though," Daisy warned. She was momentarily distracted when she watched Carly plate the cookie, and if Carly didn't know better, she'd say that the girl had nearly licked her lips.

"Oh?" Carly told herself that she was just making conversation. The child was lonely, and this was a small town where people shared their whereabouts, their routines, and their plans. It wasn't like she was taking an interest in Nick. She was just being...friendly.

She took a container of milk from the small fridge and poured a glass for Daisy. "Is your dad's shift ending soon?"

To her disappointment, the little girl shook her head. "My grandma's going to pick me up and take me to my dance class."

"I see." But inside, her heart was hammering. She had always liked Mrs. Sutton, but seeing her would only stir up all those memories that she and Nick had danced around last night. Moments that were part of the past and probably better kept there.

Definitely better kept there.

"Well, I hope you enjoy the cookie."

"Oh, I will. I wish I knew how to bake cookies like this."

Carly knew that Nick wasn't much of a baker. She'd tried to teach him—once—on a rainy June day when she was closing up and their evening plans for a picnic at the pond were disrupted. But he'd eaten more of the batter than even she did, and by the time they were finished mixing everything together, there was barely enough to make a cookie for each of them.

"It's not so hard if you have a recipe and all the ingredients," Carly started to say, but Daisy was shaking her head forcefully.

"It's hard for my dad," she said. "Last time we tried to make chocolate chip cookies they looked like pancakes."

Carly stifled a laugh. "It's actually a common problem. Here's a tip: make sure your butter isn't too soft."

"I'll tell my dad, but I'm not sure it will help. We have a class party on Thursday and I'm the only kid not bringing something homemade."

"I seem to remember your grandmother being pretty good in the kitchen," Carly said with a fond smile. "Can she help?"

Daisy shook her head, pouting. "She has too many piano lessons this week."

"Where is your contribution coming from then?" Carly asked.

"Here, of course." Daisy collected her cookie and glass of milk with a shrug.

"Well, I'll be right here if you need anything," Carly said. She watched for a moment as Daisy settled into a table nearest the counter, pulling out a notebook and some colored pencils before setting her backpack on the spare chair and then wasting no time biting into the cookie. She swung her legs underneath her while she started drawing a picture with her right hand, holding onto the cookie with her left.

Carly tried to imagine Nick as the parent to this sweet child. Coming home each day to cook her dinner, waking to get her off to school. Even attempting to make cookies with her—which was a sight she couldn't really envision but would love to see.

The bells over the door jingled again, and Carly looked over to see her oldest friend walk through the door.

"Carly! So it's true! You are back!" Joanna Newman's expression transformed from one of impatience to pure joy almost faster than Carly could process that her oldest friend was standing right in front of her.

"Joanna!" Carly squealed and thought about hoisting herself onto the counter so she could hop over it, but then thought again and ran around the side of the display case instead. Jill would have a fit if she saw Carly jumping over the counter like she did as a kid—and Carly wasn't exactly sure she could lug her adult weight over it, either.

Joanna met her at the opening of the counter, doing a little happy dance with her arms spread wide, and they immediately hugged long and tight.

It wasn't until Carly pulled away that she saw Daisy giving them a funny but curious look.

"I didn't know adults acted like that," she said, which sent Carly and Joanna into laughter.

"That's because when we're together we're not really adults," Joanna explained. "We're still ten years old and ready for our next playdate."

Now Daisy just shook her head, muttered something under her breath, and went back to her cookie.

"Speaking of, when is our next playdate?" Joanna teased. "I can't believe you're back in town and you didn't tell me!"

"And I can't believe you didn't hear until this morning," Carly laughed, knowing how word traveled around this town.

"Except I didn't hear it from you." Joanna gave her a stern look.

Carly knew her friend wasn't really mad, but she felt the need to explain.

"It was last minute, and I've only been back a couple of days, and...it's been a little crazy." She shifted her eyes toward the kitchen door, knowing Joanna would get the hint.

Sure enough, she gave a slow nod. "I see. Well, all the more reason to catch up. And the nice thing about adult playdates is that there's always wine. At least at my house!"

"That sure sounds like a weird playdate," Daisy said from a few feet away.

"Well, we are adults. Whether it feels like it or not," Carly said, giving Joanna's arm a little squeeze.

"We've been friends since we were about your age," Joanna told Daisy.

Daisy looked at them both with wide eyes, as if trying to imagine how this was even possible. "Wow, that must have been like...the olden days."

Carly and Joanna laughed.

"It feels like yesterday though, doesn't it?" Joanna said wistfully.

Carly smiled, feeling a little nostalgic when she thought

of the sleepovers in Joanna's make-shift tent or the teenage years when they'd spend their summers at the town pool, reading magazines and working on their tans. "It does. And it doesn't feel like it's been four years since we've last seen each other either."

"That's the sign of a true friend," Joanna said sagely.

"It seems I've missed out on some major things that have been happening in town these past few years," Carly said, giving a subtle glance toward Daisy. "And we do talk on the phone at least once a couple of times a month." She opened her eyes wide to underscore the point.

Joanna gave her a look of apology. "I didn't think you'd want me to bring it up. You have a busy life in Philadelphia. I guess I thought that the past was...in the past."

"It is," Carly blurted, blinking quickly. "Of course it is. I mean, that was...ancient history."

"Totally," Joanna deadpanned. All too soon, the corners of her eyes crinkled. "But here you both are, in town, at the same time, single, at the same time."

Carly shook her head but she couldn't hide her smile. She could argue the point, but luckily she was spared by the jingle of the bell.

And Nick's mother.

"Carly Parker!" Mrs. Sutton's smile was so warm that Carly couldn't feel anything but happy at the sight of her.

"Mrs. Parker!" She walked over and gave the woman a big hug.

"Please. We're all adults now. Call me Trish." Trish Sutton's deep-brown eyes crinkled when she smiled, just like her son.

"I've met your beautiful granddaughter," Carly told her. "You must be very proud."

The look on Trish's face made that much clear. "There's nothing like having my family back in town. Your grandmother must feel the exact same. Are you staying long?"

Carly shook her head regretfully. "Only through next week."

Next week. Already that felt so close. And she wasn't any closer to even starting her article, much less finishing it.

Or saving this bakery.

The day's leftovers were going to the senior center, making it easier to stomach just how many items hadn't sold that day.

Carly offered to drop them off because it was clear that Jill wasn't going to let her prep for a second night in a row, not after last night.

It was just as well. She was tired but her mind was busy. And she had the sense that Jill needed to work out some of her troubles with a rolling pin—it was great therapy, and free too, unless you counted the calories, as Nana liked to say.

The lobby of the building was small but inviting with soft piano music in the background and a crackling fire in the hearth where several of the residents were gathered around it, knitting.

It made her think of her own grandmother, who was probably back at the house, waiting for her, and she quickened her step, only pausing when she saw a familiar figure coming down the hallway.

"Nick?" Carly left the bakery boxes on the reception desk and walked over to him, her heart picking up speed when his mouth curved into a slow smile.

"Well, this is a surprise." His eyes shone with sincerity.

It was a surprise. Even though it was a small town, she hadn't expected to see him here.

"I just saw Daisy and your mother at the bakery a little bit ago. I assumed you were working tonight. Unless?" She looked around for any hint of emergency but the lobby was quiet and peaceful.

"I was visiting my grandfather on my shift break," Nick said.

"Ah." Carly couldn't help but smile when she thought of the old man who always had a sweet tooth for their cherry hand pies, especially the ones with the extra thick and sticky sugar glaze. "If I'd known, I would have baked up a batch of his favorites. We may have some treats he likes in the boxes I left with reception, though."

"I should have come over and placed an order." Nick looked as regretful as she felt. "It would have cheered up the man and given you some business."

"Well, you're already a big supporter of the bakery. And Daisy is my favorite customer." Carly grinned. "Daisy told me you were placing an order for her upcoming class party."

"Ah." Nick grinned. "Busted."

"Well, I'd never turn away business." Especially now. "But I got the sense that Daisy was hoping to bake something." She paused for a moment, hoping that she wasn't overstepping. "I'm happy to help. Teach her a recipe? The bakery is closed Wednesdays. Maybe after school tomorrow..."

"I'm off tomorrow," Nick said.

Meaning that there was no reason for Daisy to need a place to go after school. That the offer of a baking lesson in the closed kitchen wouldn't be useful.

"But if you really don't mind—" He gave her a questioning look.

"Oh. Not at all!" She wondered if that sounded too eager, but the grin in his eyes told her she didn't need to worry.

"Well, since we're both free tomorrow, maybe you could come to our place? Unless you think the bakery would be better." His mouth twitched. "That is unless you've been banned from the kitchen."

She swatted him and the brief physical contact gave her a little jolt. "Thanks for not telling Jill, by the way."

He gave her a rueful smile. "I'm not a tattletale. And technically, you're family, and it's a family business, so the policy was...grey area."

Grey area. Just like what was happening between them. They made way for two women to pass and then started to move toward the front door.

"Is it pathetic that at my age I'm still worried about getting in trouble with my older sister?" Carly mused.

"Well, Jill can be pretty intense when it comes to the bakery." Nick raised his eyebrows and Carly burst out laughing.

"She can be!" she insisted.

"Oh, I know. Do you remember the time you accidentally only added half the mixture to that pie?"

Carly groaned. How could she forget? It was one of the few times she'd let Nick into the kitchen—and come to think of it, the last.

"I thought we were making two pies, so I saved half the filling. I'll never forget the look in her eyes when she saw the bowl on the counter halfway through the baking process."

"Neither will I." Nick laughed. "I think she blamed me for distracting you."

Carly gave him a little smile. "That might have been why you weren't invited back again."

"That and I did like to steal the cookie batter," he said with a laugh.

Carly shook her head as they stepped out into the cool evening air. The days were growing longer and the lampposts glowed in the dusk. "And I thought Nana was the stickler. Jill is just as stubborn."

"I take it you haven't volunteered my services to her yet, then," Nick said, and that little bubble of hope rose again.

Carly stopped walking for a moment and looked up at him, then immediately realized her error. The dark eyes locked with hers, making it difficult to break away, to feel like there was anything outside of this small space that they shared.

But there was. An entire world outside of Nick. And she had an entire life that didn't include him.

"I wasn't sure if you really meant it," she said, a little breathlessly.

He frowned. "Of course I meant it. You know I'm a man of my word."

As soon as he said it, he looked down. Carly took a deep breath, trying not to think of all the plans they'd once had. The ones that had never happened.

"Yes," she said quietly. "You are." Because he hadn't broken a promise to her, not really.

"So what's stopping you?"

"I guess I'm afraid that if I bring it up, she'll say no. That her pride will get in the way. And the need to protect all those family recipes." Carly shook her head. "But I'm not sure what will happen if things don't change soon."

Now Nick looked concerned. "It's that bad?"

Carly swallowed hard. She wasn't ready to share the news about the potential sale. Doing so would make it all feel too real. But she couldn't keep pretending that nothing was going on either.

"I think my sisters are struggling to know what to do with the bakery now that Nana's stepped back from it," she said. "They're thinking it might be the time for them to step away too."

"But they love that bakery," he said.

"They do," Carly agreed. She thought of what Becca had said. "And Jill loves it most of all. But it's a business. I don't think this is a personal decision."

"All the more reason for me to offer my help." Before she could protest, he added, "On the house."

"On the house? But Nick, you have a job. And a daughter. I can't take your time."

"We'll make a fair trade, then. You help Daisy bake

cookies for her class party, and I help Sunrise Bakery make it into the next generation."

"That hardly seems like a fair trade to me," Carly said ruefully.

"It does to me," Nick said simply. "Daisy is the most important thing to me in the world. Just like that bakery is to you. What's life without family?"

Well, when he put it like that, Carly didn't see how she could say no. And she certainly didn't want to.

"I still have to run it by Jill..."

But Nick didn't look deterred. "I'll see you tomorrow then?"

"Tomorrow," she said. And as she walked back to her car she realized that she was looking forward to it. More than she probably should.

Even though the bakery was closed the next morning and she had every reason to sleep in, or relax and catch up with her grandmother for a few hours, Carly couldn't overlook the point of her visit. Or forget it.

Her editor hadn't either, and Carly checked her email to see that her inbox had piled up in the days since she'd been away, reminding her not just of her life outside of Hope Hollow, but of the reason for her being here at all.

She had less than two weeks before she had to return to Philadelphia with an article about the success of a small-town bakery in her hand. Something heartwarming. Something emotional. Something inspiring.

And less than two weeks to try to turn around a bakery that her family was willing to give up on.

After a quick breakfast with Nana, she parked herself at the coffeehouse on the opposite end of town from the bakery, hoping to find a fresh spin on her story idea, but after an hour of staring at a blank screen, all she had to show for her time was a cold, watery coffee that she didn't intend to finish.

This establishment didn't compete with Sunrise Bakery. For starters, there was no food served here, just beverages. It was one of the things that Carly had both loved and loathed about her hometown growing up—that there was one of everything, no other options unless you wanted to drive to the next town over. One pizza place, one bookstore, one flower shop, one diner, one grocery store, and of course, one bakery.

She perked up slightly when she saw Joanna pushing through the door bringing with her a rush of cool, spring air.

"Come sit! I didn't know you came here?"

"Only when I'm desperate," Joanna admitted. "So that usually means Wednesdays when Sunrise is closed. I have a short break before I need to get back to the shop. Let me grab that coffee and then I'll join you."

Carly was happy for the excuse to pack up her laptop and notebook. She scooted her chair to make room for Joanna as she sat down.

"So...tell me everything." Joanna sipped her coffee and then grimaced. "I don't know why I bother with this stuff."

"Probably because you were up until two in the morning reading the latest bestseller and then you had to get up early for a run before opening the bookstore?"

Joanna couldn't fight her smile. "You know me too well. But I'm not here to talk about myself. My life is predictable. You know how it is here."

Yes, Carly did. Only time and distance had given her a new appreciation for it. Instead of windows facing alleys, her bedroom at her grandmother's house faced a large maple tree and a view of Nana's lovely flowering garden, which came more alive each day. And instead of long days at the office, glued to a chair and staring at the glow of a computer screen, she was interacting with old neighbors and classmates, and the hours flew by when she was in the kitchen, kneading bread or rolling out dough, following the recipes her mother had made, and Nana's mother, too.

"How has it been being back?" Joanna pushed aside her coffee and gave Carly her full attention.

"In town or at the bakery?" Carly asked, even though she knew what her friend was getting at—she was talking about Nick, of course. But first things first. "Did you know my grandmother retired?"

Joanna winced. "Everyone knew, hon."

"Then why didn't you tell me?" Carly asked, even though she already knew the answer.

"It wasn't my news to tell. I figured that Becca or even your grandmother would tell you when they wanted you to know." Joanna's eyes looked sad. "I'm sorry."

"There's nothing to apologize for," Carly said, shaking her head. "I guess I sort of assumed that she'd be there forever." But she knew in her heart that was just wishful thinking, maybe even denial. Thinking of Nana no longer being at the bakery made her think of the other person who should be there and wasn't.

Her mother had shown up to work every day until her final week of life. And for months afterward, the kitchen had been silent, and the music stopped. The laughter too. Her apron hung on the hook, reminding them all that she should be there, but wasn't. Or that maybe a part of her still was.

Some days, Carly didn't know which was worse.

She felt the prickle of tears and she couldn't blink them away. Joanna reached out and squeezed her hand.

"I know how close you are to your grandmother. But it doesn't have to change just because she's not in the bakery every day, does it?"

"In theory, no," Carly said with a sigh. She brushed aside her remaining tears. "We're still following her recipes, still doing everything the way she did it. But..."

She paused to look around the room, making sure that they weren't overheard. The college-aged kid working the counter was too engrossed in his phone to bother with what she had to say.

Too engrossed in his phone to make a decent cup of coffee either.

Still, she leaned forward, and Joanna did the same.

"Jo." She knew that she could tell her friend anything and that it would stay between them. "My sisters are thinking of selling the bakery."

Joanna's expression mirrored Carly's original shock. "What? But why? They love working there! Don't they?"

"I thought they did." She paused for a minute, picturing her sisters' tired but satisfied faces each morning when they worked in the kitchen, sometimes laughing, other times quiet. It was good honest work, and if they weren't doing it, she wasn't sure what they'd be doing.

She wasn't so sure that they knew either.

"I think they still do. But things have apparently been a

struggle for a while. Selling might be the only option when it comes to thinking about their future."

"Selling! I had no idea things were this bad!" Joanna firmed her mouth. "I'm going to place an order for a dozen cookies. Today."

Carly gave her friend a weary smile. "Thank you, but sadly, it wouldn't be enough. I just feel so guilty. I wish I had known before things got to this point!"

"And what could you have done about it? You have a career in a city that's hours away," Joanna pointed out.

It was far from a career, but that had always been the plan. Work her way up, and she thought she was doing just that. Now, she wondered if she should be spending her energy thinking of a new article to pitch instead.

Or looking for a new job.

"I'm trying to think of how I could help. I'm supposed to be writing an article on the bakery. Small-town charm, the taste of home, the joy of a family business, that type of thing. But how can I even pull it off without being dishonest?"

Or when the bakery might be gone by the time the article was printed.

"Could the article help?" Joanna looked more optimistic than Carly felt.

"I thought so at first, but now don't see how it could. Not in time, at least."

Joanna sighed and then looked at her watch, her shoulders sagging with disappointment. "I need to get back to the bookstore. Story hour starts soon, and if I don't get the circle set up in time, I'll have toddlers running all over the room."

She pushed back her chair and paused. "Why don't you come over later? I'm closing at five today."

"Actually, I'm a little busy later on this afternoon," Carly said slowly.

Joanna didn't pick up on anything, but she had that quiet way of waiting until Carly told her all her secrets, which she knew that Carly eventually would do.

"I'm actually going over to Nick's house," Carly confessed.

"No!" Joanna's smile was wide. She glanced to the door with bright eyes and then leaned into the table eagerly. "Tell me everything."

"I thought you had to get the circle set up?" Carly reminded her.

Joanna brushed a hand through the air. "I'll make the kids do it. Put them to work for a change."

Carly couldn't help but laugh. "Well, I'm afraid that there's nothing to tell. Daisy needs some cookies for a school party and instead of buying them from the bakery, I offered to bake them with her."

"But Nick will be there?"

"I assume so." Carly gave her friend a rueful look. "But what does it matter? We're just two people who used to know each other."

"Two people who might have had an entire life together if things had been different," Joanna said, pointing out what Carly had tried to forget a long time ago.

"I'm leaving in less than two weeks. And Nick is here to stay."

Joanna conceded with a nod. "I know. I've probably

been reading too many of the romance novels we have in stock." She gave a little smile. "You have an entire life far away from here."

Carly didn't argue, even though she struggled to agree.

Her life in the city was based around a dead-end job and a promotion that would likely never happen now. Without that, what did she have keeping her there?

Or really, what did she have keeping her from moving back here?

"And here I was having visions of you and Nick rekindling your romance over a bowl of batter." Joanna's sigh was wistful.

Now Carly really laughed. "Now I *know* that you've been reading too many books from the romance section."

"What can I say? I've been engaged to my high school sweetheart for enough years that our mothers are starting to wish we *had* eloped."

"You still haven't settled on a date?" Carly asked, even though she knew the answer. Michael was doing his residency at the hospital and they'd decided to wait until things settled down and they had more time.

"For now I'm content as I am. We're like an old married couple by now anyway. So I'm living vicariously through your exciting life."

"Sorry to let you down, but my life is far from exciting. Especially my love life," Carly added.

Now, Joanna looked coy. "So there's really been *no* one interesting in Philly?"

Carly thought about this for about half a second. The

handful of dates she'd gone on in recent years had been boring at best. "Nope."

Joanna's eyes lit up. "See? All the more reason for you and Nick—"

But Carly shook her head, silencing that thought, even if she had entertained it herself each time she left his company. It was so easy to be with Nick, just like it always had been.

"Things change," Joanna said as she stood and tossed her paper cup still full of coffee into the nearest bin.

They certainly did, Carly thought. But not enough for her to get her hopes up when it came to Nick Sutton.

Nick didn't know who was looking more forward to Carly's visit—he or his daughter. She'd been talking about it ever since he picked her up from school, excited that she'd have the best cookies at the party because one of the "Sunrise Sisters" was going to be baking them with her.

He pushed back a wave of apprehension. It had been years since Liz's announcement that she needed to "find herself" and "work on herself", and even though Daisy had adjusted and was rarely seen without a smile on her face, he was there for the confusion, the questions, about why they were moving and her mother wasn't joining them. He saw the way his daughter's eyes still lit up every time Liz called or sent an overpriced gift. Guilt gifts, that's what he called them.

And he also wiped away the tears when Liz left again.

The visits were both good and bad, and for this reason,

he hadn't told Daisy yet about Liz's intentions. He'd wait until there were actual plans—and then brace himself for the fallout when she left again.

He hated the way Liz sailed in and out of their lives as much as Daisy craved it. Hated that he couldn't protect his daughter from the inevitable disappointment. But he could protect her against more hurt.

And for that reason, he hoped that she didn't become too attached to Carly.

He told himself that it was just cookie-baking. That Daisy was friendly with almost everyone in town. That this was no different.

But it felt different, to him, and when the doorbell rang at four and he walked down the hallway to see Carly standing behind the glass-paned door, smiling back at him, he realized that the heart that really needed protecting was his own.

She was just in town for a visit. And he was here to stay.

He opened the door. The vision of her standing on his front stoop felt strange but right all at the same time. How many times after first moving back to Hope Hollow had he kept an eye out for her, passing by all their old favorite spots, happy for any reports her family was willing to share?

But she never came back to town and eventually, he stopped believing she ever would.

Now, he realized he'd never stopped hoping.

"Hello," he said, welcoming her inside. He ran his gaze over her as she set her bag down on the bench where Daisy always sat to tie her shoes. Carly's light brown hair fell at her shoulders, gracing her collarbone, and the green top she wore brought out hints of the same color in her eyes.

"What a cute house!"

He gave a modest shrug. "It's small but it works."

"It has window boxes," Carly added.

Nick rolled back on his heels. "I know." And that was the first thing he'd said when he'd seen the listing. It was what had drawn him to this place. He'd never noticed details like that before, but whenever he was out with Carly, she made sure to point them out.

Being with Carly always made him feel like he was right where he was meant to be. And somehow, this house made him feel the same way.

Carly poked her head into the front living room, where Daisy had been watching a cartoon.

Now, Daisy bounded off the couch and into the entryway. "You're here! We're going to bake cookies!"

"I know!" Carly laughed and, before Nick had time to say anything more, allowed Daisy to take her by the hand and all but run her into the kitchen at the back of the house.

Per Daisy's insistence, Nick had purchased every baking staple he could think of this morning.

"Did we get enough supplies?" Daisy asked. "The sprinkles were my idea. Pink, of course."

"Of course." Carly gave a serious nod to Daisy and then turned to give him a slow smile. "I can see you were prepared for this."

Not in the least. Nick often felt like he hadn't been prepared for anything in his life—not Daisy coming into his life. Not Carly strolling back into it ten years after he'd tried to push her out of his mind.

"You know me. Always trying to get things right."

They locked eyes for a moment, and then Nick cleared his throat. "Well, I have to say that I'm pretty hopeless in the kitchen—"

Carly laughed. "Oh, I remember." She leaned down and stage-whispered to Daisy, "Your dad once put a full cup of salt into the cookie batter instead of sugar."

"I seem to recall that you nearly burned down the bakery last week," Nick teased.

"Touché. Although, it would never have gotten that far. Not with the alarm. Or you on call."

He saw a blush rise up in her cheeks as she glanced away.

"My dad is very brave," Daisy said solemnly.

"Luckily there hasn't been anything serious to worry about," Nick said, knowing that Daisy loved to tell people he was a firefighter because it sounded so much more important than the management consulting job he had back in Boston. It was in many ways of course, but a lot of the days were quieter than he might have expected.

Everything about life here was quieter. And looking at his daughter, he was reminded of why that mattered. Why, maybe, it was better.

"Being back here suits you," Carly observed as if reading his thoughts.

He grinned. "It does. And Daisy likes it here, too."

Suddenly Daisy frowned. "I miss my mom, though. She didn't come with us when we moved."

Carly's eyes met his, and this time, it was she who cleared

her throat.

"Should we start making these cookies, Daisy? I happen to have a recipe with me for something called..." She made a big production of shuffling through her handbag and finding a folded piece of paper. "Unicorn cookies?"

Daisy's eyes burst open and she squealed when she grabbed the colored sprinkles from the table and ran them over to the kitchen island.

"You're really good with kids," Nick said.

Carly shrugged away the compliment. "I'm one of three girls. I know a thing or two about what girls like at this age."

Nick could only push back his usual twinge of guilt when he saw the way his daughter's eyes were lit up. "I wish I had that instinct."

Carly gave him a funny look, but they didn't talk about anything other than cookies, recipes, and Daisy's favorite flavors until the cookies were safely out of the oven, cooled, and decorated.

"Can I go call Grandma and tell her about the cookies?" Daisy asked, already running out of the room.

"I hope your mother won't think it's strange that I'm here," Carly said, watching her go.

Nick just shook his head. "My mother will be happy you're here. She likes you, you know. And she always felt..." He trailed off. His mother had felt the same way he had all those years ago when he was faced with an impossible decision. Or maybe not a decision at all.

Carly was watching him carefully. "It was a complicated situation. For what it's worth, Nick, I want you to know that I don't have hard feelings. You made the right choice."

"I wish I felt that way sometimes," he said, raising his eyebrows.

"You don't have to tell me what happened," Carly said, but her expression was open and caring, and he knew that she wasn't shutting down the topic because she was uncomfortable. They were past all that by now. Carly had moved away. Moved on.

Now, he wondered if she'd ever found a greater love in the years since they'd been together.

Because he hadn't. Not romantically, at least, he thought, thinking of Daisy.

"It feels weird to be talking to you about this when…"

"When we broke up so you could go back to her?" Carly sighed and then gave him a kind smile. "It was a long time ago. And you were going to be a father. I understand, Nick. And seeing you with Daisy…I wouldn't have changed a thing, and I don't think you would have either."

"No, I wouldn't have." He was sure of that. It was everything else that was so confusing. Had he been right, getting married to a woman he didn't fully love and who didn't love him? He told himself he was, but Liz was the one who said otherwise, in the weeks and months leading up to their split.

"Things worked out the way were meant to," Carly said, and her smile was so genuine that for a second he almost believed her.

She was right in so many ways. But when he tucked his little girl into bed at night and she asked about her mother, he couldn't help but feel like nothing had worked out as he'd intended at all.

"Liz." He paused at the sound of his ex-wife's name.

"She wasn't happy and hadn't been for a long time. Maybe neither of us was. We thought we could make it work, and for a long time, we did. For me, it was enough, having Daisy. I was content to go to work, come home, and enjoy family life. I still am." He grinned.

"I can tell it suits you," Carly said with a smile that told him it was okay to keep going.

"But the hours were long and some days I had to ask myself what I was doing."

Carly nodded. "I get that."

"I guess Liz did too. She started feeling restless, started finding new hobbies, reasons to be out of the house. She was meeting new people. She was doing all the things she felt she had missed out on, I guess. And we started arguing a lot. How she was never home. How Daisy missed her." Nick shook his head. Even now, it bothered him to reflect on that time. "Looking back, she was trying to find balance, but in all the wrong ways. She hadn't planned on this life, and I think she had more regrets than I did. Not about Daisy but about getting married. Forcing something that wasn't there. She wanted to see what else life could offer her."

"Where is she now?"

"At this moment? Who knows. She travels a lot for work. Goes out to dinners at nice restaurants." He sighed. "She visits Daisy, but not often. She sends gifts. But doing the daily work that comes with parenting, not anymore. Maybe she never did. It's not glamorous or exciting. But I wouldn't trade it for the world."

"Her loss then," Carly said, and for a moment, their eyes

met. Nick didn't know if she was referring to Daisy or him, but he wasn't about to read into it.

Besides, Carly was right. It was Liz's loss. But in so many ways, it was Daisy's too.

"Everything I do is to make Daisy happy. Her happiness brings me happiness."

"That's the way it should be. And she is happy, at least from what I see. And you are too. I can tell." Carly's smile was both warm and a little sad.

He was. And he wanted to believe that Daisy was too. But there were always those moments that made him wonder what more he could have done, what he could have done differently.

"There's nothing I wouldn't do for her."

"Even bake cookies!" Carly laughed. "You in an apron is something I never thought I'd see."

"Oh, then you haven't seen me in a tiara when it's time for high tea with the stuffed animals."

Now Carly's eyes popped. "You're kidding!"

"I wish I was," he said bashfully. But that wasn't true, was it? He wouldn't give up those tea parties for any night out with the guys, or a swanky vacation.

Not even for a moment longer with the girl standing in front of him, reminding him what it felt like to be in love.

"I just wish I had known back then what I know now," he said quietly.

She laughed. "Don't we all?"

He frowned at her now, wondering if she was content with her choices in life. Maybe, she was just thinking about the bakery.

"Well, this was nice," Carly said, looping her handbag over her shoulder. "But I should probably get home and see my grandmother."

Reluctantly, he walked her back to the front door, wondering if he should ask her to stay, or if she wanted him to. He decided not to push it. and before he could change his mind and do something to ruin a nice afternoon, he pulled open the door. She stepped out onto the front porch and turned to give him one last smile.

It took him back to a day he'd tried to forget. The day they'd broken up, when he'd had to tell her the truth, that his world had changed in an instant, and that every plan, every hope they'd had together, had ended.

He'd expected her to be angry, but instead, she'd been silent. There was nothing to say, and looking back, he knew that now.

He'd wanted to kiss her, one last time, but he knew that he couldn't do that to her. Or to Liz. Or to himself.

Now, he felt that same pull. That urge to reach out, bring her back to him, hold her close.

But now, like then, he resisted.

"It was. Daisy had a great time." And so had he. "And I haven't forgotten our deal."

Now, Carly's smile slipped. "I don't know..."

"I get off early tomorrow. Why don't I stop in, later in the day, just to...check things out?"

Carly hesitated and then nodded. "It can't hurt."

Technically, it couldn't. But seeing Carly again, knowing that soon she'd be gone again... Well, that was bittersweet.

ten

Carly was admittedly watching the clock right before Daisy pushed through the bakery door the next afternoon, the grin on her face nearly as big as her backpack.

"How did it go?" Carly asked, leaning into her elbows on the counter.

Daisy's eyes gleamed. "Everyone liked my cookies the best! I tried to save you one, but the other kids gobbled them all up."

Carly grinned. "That's okay. We made them so everyone could enjoy them. And I probably eat too many sweets anyway."

Daisy looked wistfully at the display case. "I wish I could have another one. Why don't you sell them here?"

Carly glanced at Nick, who had been slower to walk through the door. Her stomach swooped a little when he flashed her a smile that spread all the way to his eyes.

"Well, we only make my grandmother's recipes here. That cookie recipe was something I created myself."

"That's too bad," Daisy said. "I bet all my friends would ask their parents to bring them here all the time for those cookies!"

"Yeah," Nick said, squinting thoughtfully. "I bet they would."

Carly shrugged it off. "Them's the rules. We bake our grandmother's secret recipes. The same ones we've been making since she was a little girl. Technically, that would make them our great-grandmother's recipes, but we just think of them as Nana's."

Nick looked thoughtful as Daisy continued to chatter. "I've decided that when I grow up, I want to be a baker. I want to work in a place just like this."

Carly laughed, flattered, but then a thought struck her. Would her sisters and grandmother feel more optimistic about the fate of Sunrise Bakery if they knew that there was a future generation to carry on the legacy?

She glanced at Becca, who was helping another customer with a cake order for an upcoming anniversary party, wondering if her sister ever felt that pressure, or regret. She'd been engaged, planning an entire life with Jonah. One that had probably included a couple of children, knowing Becca.

Carly swallowed hard and forced a smile at Daisy. There was no point in living life thinking about what might have been, even if she was guilty of it herself. Especially now.

"I think that you would be an excellent baker," she told Nick's daughter. "Now, your usual or would you like to try something different today? A raspberry bar, perhaps?"

Daisy seemed to waver and then, hesitantly, asked, "Can I have both?"

Carly laughed. "Only if I don't get in trouble with your dad." She glanced at Nick, feeling that usual pang that accompanied that strange mixture of attraction and loss.

"So it's up to me to be the bad guy?" He was joking, but there was sadness in his gaze when their eyes met.

"Never," she said quietly.

"Please, Dad? Just this once?" Daisy asked.

Carly gave him a pleading look. "It's just this once." She'd be a terrible mother, spoiling her kids, probably rotting their teeth in the process with all the sweets they'd eat.

She pondered that as she plated a raspberry bar with a crumble topping and then the oatmeal cookie she'd set aside. She'd never thought about kids, not seriously really. She'd been too focused on her career, the life she was building for herself in Philly. Family, both past and future, hadn't been at the forefront of her mind.

Until now.

With a pull in her chest, she handed over the plate with two cookies to Daisy and started to pour the milk. As usual, Daisy added her dollar bills to the tip jar, and Carly let her because right now they needed all the help they could get. Plus, she had a feeling that Daisy felt important adding money to the jar.

Nick, however, pulled out his wallet and slapped down a few bills that covered the tab and then some.

"Because we'll be loitering for a bit," he said, his tone showing that he wasn't going to take no for an answer.

"You wouldn't be the first," Carly said lightly after Nick instructed Daisy to find a seat at a table near the window.

"We get some people in here who sit for hours, working on their computers, or reading."

Nick's brow pinched a little. "Regulars, I take it?"

Carly nodded, thinking of some of the faces she'd seen over the week. Most of them were the same people she remembered coming in daily back when she still lived in town.

"Loyal customers," she said with a smile.

Nick, however, didn't seem to see it that way. "Loyal, perhaps. Patrons, yes. But if they're just ordering one pastry and a cup of coffee, they're taking up space for new customers. You'd be surprised by how many people might walk on by if they don't think they can easily get a seat."

Carly hadn't thought of that. And she wondered if either of her sisters had. Certainly, Nana never would have seen it that way.

"This has always been the layout of the space," Nick observed, taking in the room.

Carly nodded. "It's always worked."

"How's it working now, though?" Nick asked, silencing her.

Carly pushed out a breath and turned to see that Becca was still busy with the cake order and Jill was of course back in the kitchen.

"I haven't had a chance to talk to Jill yet," she whispered. More like, she hadn't worked up the courage. She thought it might be better to see what Nick had to say and then decide if it was worth running the risk of upsetting her family with his suggestions.

So far, she was starting to think that it was.

Now Nick was describing how they could better utilize the long bench along the far wall, fit in more tables, free up some of the center space and add even more opportunities for people to sit and actually enjoy their treats rather than take them to go in a paper bag.

"You're really good at this," she remarked.

His cheeks turned a little pink as his smile grew shy. "Just comes naturally. It's what I did for years."

"And now he's a firefighter!" Daisy cut in from across the room.

"Now I'm a firefighter," Nick said with a nod. "But it doesn't mean I've forgotten everything I've learned."

"I can see that. And your ideas are good ones."

"You sound surprised," he said.

"I guess I'm more surprised that no one in my family ever thought of it themselves."

"Sometimes it's hard to see things clearly when you're too close to it," he said, locking her eyes.

She swallowed hard, feeling the pull of their connection, wanting to fight against it as much as she wanted to give in.

Things were becoming murky, and not just between them. Her once straightforward life no longer felt so clear at all.

They were interrupted by Daisy, who was springing over to the counter with a plate that didn't even bear a single crumb. "That was delicious, but I still like the unicorn cookies better."

"An honest customer!" Carly laughed.

But there was Nick, giving her that look again.

"Are you going to the Spring Carnival?" Daisy asked excitedly.

Carly smiled at the memory of the town's annual event, held every spring on the square. She looked forward to it each year, saving up her allowance money for rides on the Ferris wheel or games that she never did seem to win. It was one night a year when she and her sisters or friends could go off on their own, well past dark, the lights and music and sugar making their usual quiet downtown come to life.

Now, looking at Nick, she realized that this event had a whole new meaning for him and his daughter. Not only did the fire department plan the event, but they also benefited from the proceeds.

"When is it?" she asked, because that was one detail she couldn't remember.

"Kicks off next Friday and goes until Saturday," Nick replied.

In other words, the day before she'd be leaving for home.

Only home didn't feel like Philadelphia right now. It felt like Hope Hollow. This bakery. These people.

And Nick.

"I can't think of a better way to spend the weekend," she said with a bright smile. Even if it was a time she didn't really want to think about, not just yet.

With a heavy heart, she watched as Nick took Daisy's hand and led her outside, feeling a strange sense of nostalgia as she watched them go even though she was right here and so were they. She told herself it was the bakery, the thought of losing it, and never having a moment like this back that filled her with a sense of missing something—even though it felt a little more like a sense of missing out.

On spending more time with Nick and his daughter. On making more memories together. Right here at Sunrise Bakery.

Nick's suggestions for the bakery were still in her mind after she rang up the next few customers and Becca finally finished taking the order for the anniversary cake.

"Looks like you and Nick have been getting along," her sister mused.

Carly thought about telling Becca the real topic of their conversation but decided it wasn't the time. Besides, she and Nick *were* getting along. There was no point in arguing.

"What happened between us was a long time ago. There aren't any hard feelings." There never really was. Just heartbreak. "What happened was unavoidable and I respected his choice, even if it hurt. And who couldn't love Daisy?"

"Her mother," Becca said, and then shook her head. "Sorry. That wasn't fair of me. But it gets my back up when I see that little girl coming in here, waiting for Nick or her grandmother to take her home."

"Does she ever mention her mother?" Carly couldn't help but be curious. "She seems happy."

"All thanks to Nick. He's a wonderful father to her. I think she brings out the best in him." Becca closed her eyes. "Sorry, Carly. I don't mean to upset you."

"You're not," Carly assured her. "And I agree. Daisy is the love of Nick's life from what I can see. It makes it easier to accept why things ended between us all those years ago."

"Still, just...be careful." Becca's face was sober, a pinch

between her brows showing her worry. "I know how much you loved him and how upset you were when it ended."

Carly could still remember the pain as sharp as if it were yesterday. One day they were madly in love, the next day, everything just came to a grinding halt. No warning. Nothing to do but accept that it was over. There wasn't an argument or anyone to blame.

"Things are different now," Carly pointed out.

"Meaning you're both single?"

"Meaning that Nick's a single father living in his home-town and I'm...just visiting. Our lives went two different ways a long time ago. There's nothing more to it than that."

"But would you want there to be more?"

Carly thought about it and then stopped herself immedi-ately. Now, just like all those years ago when he'd told her they had to end things, she accepted the facts for what they were because to fight them would have only made things worse.

"It doesn't matter what I would have wanted. The reality is that in less than two weeks I'll be back at my apartment in Philly, at my job at the magazine."

Only she wasn't so sure that she'd have a job waiting for her when she got back.

Or if it was even a job she still wanted.

The bookshop was just three blocks down from the bakery, and, like Sunrise, it had been in Joanna's family for genera-tions. As a child, Carly remembered stopping in on evenings after the bakery had closed, her mother tired but content, never leaving without a purchase, even if it was usually another cookbook.

Carly thought of that now as she pushed through the door. For all the cookbooks her mother had collected over the years, she'd only ever tried those recipes at home—never introducing anything new at the bakery.

But then, that's the way traditions were, Carly supposed. And the well-worn slipcovered chairs in the corner of this bookshop were proof of that.

Joanna came in through the side door that Carly knew from being here so often over the years led to the small storage room that had once doubled as Joanna's father's office.

"Well, this is a nice surprise!"

"Thought I'd see if you wanted to grab that glass of wine tonight," Carly said. Nana had mentioned that she'd be busy this evening—not on a date with Mr. Quincy, she'd been sure to clarify.

"I'd love to, but as a member of the local commerce, I have to get over to the town hall for my planning committee meeting. You're welcome to join me. I'm sure everyone would be so excited to see you, and one of your sisters will be there to represent Sunrise Bakery."

They hadn't mentioned it, but then, Jill was still a little upset about the whole burnt cookie situation. Not to mention other, more important things.

Carly gave her friend a stern look. "The planning committee? This wouldn't happen to be for the upcoming carnival, would it?"

"Of course. It's a town event." Joanna straightened a stack of books on the counter and loaded them into her arms.

"And it benefits the fire station," Carly said pointedly.

"And I am an active member of my community." Joanna's smile was rueful as she came around the counter. "Would it be so bad to run into Nick again?"

"I don't think this would fall under bumping into him. He's going to be there," Carly said as she followed her friend into the fiction section.

Joanna set the stack of books down on a table with other candy-colored covers. "And what's so bad about that? From what I see and hear, you two are getting along as well as ever."

"See and hear?" Something clicked. "Who's been talking?"

"No one." But Joanna had never been a good liar, even when it served her. "Okay, maybe just a few people. Nick's mother got to talking to Maria and she talked to Simone and..."

"And everyone's thinking that it would be so great if Nick and I got back together because then I'd have a reason to stay." Carly's eyes burst open on a sudden thought. "Wait! That's probably what my grandmother is hoping!"

Even though she'd only been half-joking and certainly speculating, Joanna winced. "Would you blame her?" she asked, walking back to the counter.

Carly wandered over to the front of the store. "No. But I'm not going to give her false hope."

"False hope?" Joanna tsked and grabbed her handbag.

The decision had clearly been made. "Says the girl who used to try to outrun the rain clouds."

Carly laughed. "I'd nearly forgotten that!"

"Well, I haven't. I can still remember tagging along with you to the town pool, even though the forecast called for a ninety percent chance of rain within the hour."

"Hey, if the sun was still shining..." Carly shook her head. More often than not, the first raindrops would fall as soon as they set down their towels, but if they hadn't tried, they might have missed out.

She felt her smile slip when she thought about that. When had she stopped trying? With her family? With this town? With everything that had mattered so much to her?

It had snuck up on her before she'd even realized it.

Joanna gave her a little nudge. "What happened to my best friend who always saw the infinite potential in life?"

"She grew up," Carly said, a little sadly.

Because as much as she'd love to hold out hope that somehow everything could go back to the way it was, or might have been, she just couldn't set herself up for that kind of disappointment again.

If someone had told Nick five years ago that he'd be taking notes at the monthly Hope Hollow meeting, he'd have laughed. Or been worried. Or wondered where, when, and how his life went off track.

But now, he was settled in his usual chair, tonight for the special meeting called for the upcoming carnival, a cup of coffee in his hand, his friends and neighbors filling out the room.

And despite the unexpected path that had brought him here, not just tonight, but monthly, ever since he'd returned, he couldn't imagine wanting to be anywhere else.

Most of the time. He'd be lying to himself if he said he didn't feel a little jolt of energy when he was at the bakery today—and not only because he was face-to-face with Carly Parker. He'd always enjoyed his consulting career, but he enjoyed his role as a father more. And there wasn't much need for that kind of work here in Hope Hollow.

"Well, what do you know? Look who just walked in." Frankie gave him a crooked smile that could only mean one thing.

He looked up, nearly spilling his coffee when he saw Carly walk into the room, followed by Joanna. From the looks of it, they were still close, and for a moment, Nick wondered again what might have been if he'd handled things differently. If he and Carly would still be close. As friends. As more than friends.

"You guys gonna dance around your true feelings all night again? That night at the station was torture, man."

Nick turned a hard look on Frankie, who was struggling to contain his laughter.

"You could have excused yourself from the table," he told his friend.

"And let my meatballs go cold?" Frankie gave a dramatic shudder, and now Nick managed to laugh.

Still, looking back at Carly, who was settling into the back row, he swallowed hard, wondering why he was suddenly nervous, telling himself it was just that he wasn't prepared. A glance across the room was interrupted by the dramatic eyebrow raise of his mother, who more than playfully elbowed Carly's grandmother seated beside her.

Was this their doing then? It wouldn't surprise him. Nick knew how much his mother had always liked the Parker girls, or the Sunrise Sisters as she, along with the rest of the town, called them. She had never warmed to Liz but welcomed her into the family all the same, and Nick knew that his mother had to hold back her true opinions whenever she was mentioned, for Daisy's sake.

But if his mother thought that he and Carly had a second chance, she could think again. Carly was just passing through town. And he...he was committed. To this town. To his daughter. To giving her a stable life, one with no more upheaval, no more changes, even if that meant sacrificing some of his own happiness. It wouldn't be the first time.

That was the one thing that he could guarantee by moving back to Hope Hollow. A life with simple pleasures, if not a little boring. He hadn't minded it, only on the occasional Saturday night when Daisy was in bed and the house felt too quiet.

But judging by the way his chest seemed to come alive at the sight of his first love, he tried to chalk it up to his stale social life. Nothing more.

Because it could never be anything more than that.

He told himself that all through the meeting, trying to keep from looking her way, and afterward, when somehow the crowd seemed to all but push him in her direction, leaving them to walk out into the cool evening air at the exact same time.

"Didn't expect to see you tonight," he said mildly.

"Joanna convinced me," she said, motioning to her friend who had walked up ahead a few paces. "We're going to have a glass of wine, but first...business."

"Speaking of business—"

She groaned. "I haven't talked to Jill yet."

"Actually, I was going to ask if you were going to enter the bake-off." It was a tradition at the carnival for some good-natured competition.

"Oh, no. We can't ask that of Nana. Not with her arthritis." Carly looked a little sad for a moment, and Nick almost regretted bringing it up. Nana Parker entered on behalf of Sunrise Bakery every single year, and to his knowledge, she'd only lost once.

And no one dared speak of it.

"Jill hasn't mentioned it," Carly continued, but then shook her head. "But they're spread so thin. I'm sure it's the furthest thing from their mind."

"Then why not you? Those were some amazing cookies, at least according to Daisy." He grinned.

"One of my own recipes?" Carly looked shocked at the thought and then immediately shook her head.

"But why not see how it goes over with the crowd? You know you'll win over the kids." He frowned at her now, seeing the reluctance in her eyes. "Think about it. As you said, it can't hurt."

"Sometimes change does, though, doesn't it?" she said, before stepping away to join her friend.

He shoved his hands into his pocket, knowing that there was nothing he could say to that. She was right. Sometimes change hurt.

But sometimes, he thought with a little smile, it had an unexpected way of giving you exactly what you needed.

eleven

Carly prepped herself for the talk with Jill the entire walk to the bakery the next morning, but by the time Main Street came into view, even the cool morning air and the soft chirp of birds couldn't calm her nerves.

No one had ever questioned the way things were done at the bakery.

Now, she was wondering if that was just the problem.

Both of her sisters were in the kitchen when she pushed inside the space that already smelled like cinnamon and sugar. Her stomach grumbled at the familiar scent.

"Nana's cinnamon rolls?" she asked, even though she already knew the answer.

Sure enough, Jill said, "Wouldn't be a Friday morning without them."

Or a Saturday or Sunday, Carly thought to herself. It was one of many tried and true traditions here at Sunrise, where the weekend kicked off a day early.

"Are they still a big seller?" Carly asked as she looped her apron over her neck and reached for the strings at her waist.

Becca glanced at their oldest sister who was setting another tray of cinnamon rolls into the proving drawer.

"Usually," Jill replied.

In other words, not like before—when Nana was here, and there was sometimes a line out the door on a Saturday morning, especially at the first snap of cold in the air.

"Before I forget, when I saw Nana last night at the town meeting, she invited us over for dinner tomorrow," Becca told Jill. She glanced at Carly. "Unless you have other plans?"

"What kind of other plans?" Carly laughed and stepped toward the counter. Sure, it would be nice to have another dinner with Nick, but there was also no point in it. He was here and she was...there. Even though right now Philadelphia felt like another person's life, not her own.

Becca just gave her a knowing lift of an eyebrow and Jill stayed focused on her baking. There was a line of baked goods already waiting to go into the oven—a slower process given that they were down one.

"If you mean romantic plans, then I could be asking you two the same thing," Carly said, then cut a glance at Becca to make sure she hadn't hit a nerve.

But Becca just shook her head, and Jill said, "Who has time for a love life? This bakery takes up most of our hours and all of our energy."

Now, Becca's smile slipped. A nerve *had* been hit. But they both knew that Jill didn't mean it.

Carly saw a need to cut in. "Nana mentioned the same

thing to me this morning before I left. It sounds nice. We haven't all sat down together since I've been back."

"We haven't sat down to a proper meal since Nana retired," Jill said with a weary sigh. "It will be nice." She gave Carly a smile that both boosted Carly's resolve to help and also made her not want to upset this moment.

"I was surprised to see you at the town meeting last night." Becca gave her a teasing grin, meaning that she really meant she'd seen her talking to Nick. Again.

"If this is about Nick, there's nothing to share. I had plans with Joanna and she wanted to stop by so I joined her. And it's a small town. I'm bound to bump into Nick."

"Bumping into him and talking are two different things." But Becca smiled. "I'm happy you two are getting along."

"The past is in the past. No sense in holding onto it," Carly replied. Which brought her to what she really needed to say. "Nick was a management consultant in Boston. Did you know that?"

Becca gave a distracted shrug as she measured out some flour. "He's kept his conversation brief since he moved back." She glanced at Carly. "I think he worried we'd hold a grudge at first."

Like how Carly did with Jonah for leaving her sister midway through her wedding planning?

But that was a very different situation. Still, sisters were sisters and the Sunrise Sisters had each other's backs, even though Carly couldn't help but feel like she'd turned hers on them for a while.

"He has experience turning struggling businesses around," she explained. She eyed Jill across the workbench, but her sister remained focused on her task.

"Anyway," she said, feeling her heart begin to pound. "He suggested that we might move around some of the tables, and make space for more people to sit. Especially when some customers are known to linger."

Now Jill looked up. "Linger? That's because they love it here!"

Carly glanced at Becca. She could tell by the pleading look in her eyes that she had her support.

"Well," Becca said with a light laugh. "They may love it, but they also order a coffee and a muffin and then stay for half the morning."

Jill pinched her lips. There was clearly no disputing that.

"Nick thought if we utilized that bench along the far wall, we could line up more tables, then fill in the center space with others."

"That's not how Nana likes it," Jill said with a huff as if that was that. Once, it would have been. The timer went off and Jill slid on an oven mitt and retrieved a batch of cinnamon rolls from the rack. She seemed to set them down on the counter with more force than necessary. "Besides, where are we supposed to get these extra tables and chairs?"

"Maria has an entire back room full of extra tables and chairs for when they have parties," Becca pointed out. "I'm sure she'd let us use them until we can order more."

"Order more?" Jill shook her head. "With what money? We don't even have enough to buy a new oven, which is a top priority given that we run a bakery."

"But if it brings in more people..." Carly pressed gently.

"She has a point, Jill," Becca said. "More people means more sales which means a new oven."

Now Jill set her hands on her hips and looked at Carly properly. "And why do you suddenly care so much?"

"I've always cared," Carly said calmly, wondering if she'd ever be able to get Jill to understand that. "But working in this bakery was different for you."

"You've got that right." Jill shook her head. "I've always taken it seriously. Someone had to."

For the first time, Carly recognized her older sister's burden, or at least the one she believed she had to carry. Not just the legacy of this bakery, but the leadership, too. Who had been there, at Nana's side, at this very counter, right after her mother had died? And who had wiped Carly's tears and insisted, almost sternly, that everything would be okay?

Now Carly wondered if Jill had been trying to convince herself, mimicking what Nana said and did, because she didn't know any other way.

"Ever think you've taken it too seriously?" Carly asked gently. When Jill just stared at her, she continued, "I just mean that maybe it's okay to let others help once in a while. To let me help."

Jill wavered as an old argument awakened. "You've been back in town for a week and you think you can fix a problem that I haven't been able to solve for months?"

To Carly's surprise, tears sprang to Jill's eyes and she quickly brushed them away.

"I didn't mean to upset you," Carly said, coming around the counter to put an arm around her sister's shoulder. It felt weird to be the one comforting her older sister when it had always been the other way around, but she wasn't a kid anymore; she was on equal footing with both Jill and Becca. At least, she wanted to be. "I just...I want to help. I'm only in town for another week."

Another week. And two days. But already the time was slipping by. And so was this bakery.

"We may as well try," Becca said, her tone a question, meaning that she too was looking for Jill to give her approval.

"But Nana..." Jill's voice trailed away.

"Will be more upset to have no bakery at all," Becca said firmly. "Jill, I don't think we have a choice."

"Just give me through next week to see if I can help," Carly jumped in, seeing an opportunity.

Jill blinked rapidly and then went back to her mixing bowl. "Okay," she said. "But Nana isn't going to like this."

"I'll give Maria a call!" Becca announced, the excitement high in her voice as she moved toward the office where the landline was still mounted on the wall. "I'm sure Frankie can have those extra tables brought over before we open today."

Carly could barely fight her smile when she met Becca's bright eyes.

A week to try to make a difference. To set things right.

And hope that Nana didn't stop by until things were better. Or Carly was long gone.

~

Dinner the next night wasn't fancy, but then Nana always said that her skills in the kitchen didn't extend to the stovetop.

"It's a perfect night to eat in the garden," Nana said with a smile while she prepared the pie that would accompany the pasta salad Carly had made that afternoon. Nana had insisted on making the dessert, and Carly didn't try to stop her. Besides, Nana wouldn't have listened anyway.

"Why don't you snip some flowers for a centerpiece?" Nana suggested.

Carly didn't see a reason for such formality, but she was happy for the task. She walked out into the garden, breathing in the cool, fragrant scent, and surveyed her grandmother's perennial beds. It was early spring and much was yet to bloom. The peonies were always her favorite, but they were still several weeks off.

She decided to take some of the new daffodils, a favorite of hers as a child.

She was just bending down to clip some from the edge of the yard when the sound of laughter pulled her attention up and, conveniently enough, to the hole in the hedge. She leaned forward, just shy of pressing her face against the rough greens of the arborvitae, and took in the sight. A slightly obstructed view of Frannie's patio was visible, and Frannie herself sat at the table, sipping wine, laughing at something a gentleman was saying.

Had Frannie found love? Carly's interest was piqued as she leaned in closer, to see if she could hear anything, but one peal of laughter was followed by another and Frannie only stopped to take another sip of her wine. The man was laughing too if the shake of his shoulders said anything, and Carly had nearly given up seeing who had finally won Frannie's heart when the woman started to stand and the man gestured for her to stay, getting up himself.

"Mr. Quincy!" Carly gasped, then covered her mouth.

"Boo!" a voice whispered in her ear, so close to her skin that it would have prickled if she hadn't yelped and jumped instead.

She turned, her heart pounding under her palm, to see Nick staring at her with gleaming eyes.

"What—what are you doing?" she gasped.

"I could ask you the same thing," he said, barely hiding his amusement. "You weren't spying on someone through the hedge, were you?"

"What? No!" As if! But Carly wasn't sure she had convinced Nick any more than she could be sure that Mr. Quincy himself hadn't caught her in the act.

"I was...picking flowers." She gestured to the daffodils at her feet and quickly picked them up. "For a centerpiece. We're about to have dinner."

"I know." Nick held up a bottle of wine.

Oh. Oh, no she hadn't! "Did...Becca invite you?" Nana had surprisingly never mentioned Nick being back in town or the many run-ins that she surely knew Carly had shared with him.

"Your grandmother, actually," he replied with a grin.

Carly could only shake her head. So this was how her grandmother was going to play it. She should have known she was up to something.

"I ran into her today at the market and she insisted I come. Wouldn't take no for an answer, actually."

"Is Daisy here too?" Carly looked around. It was easier with Nick's daughter around. It reminded her of her place. Their circumstances. Of reality.

But Nick shook his head. "Birthday party. I don't pick her up until eight. Your grandmother saw me buying a frozen pizza and all but snatched it from my hand."

Carly laughed. "I still can't bring myself to admit to her how much frozen pizza I consume."

"Here I figured you'd be eating out in all those great restaurants the city has to offer."

"That would require someone to eat them with," Carly said, then, catching the raise of his eyebrow, she blushed. "I mean...my friends work long hours too, and by the end of the day I'm tired and..."

And she may as well have plastered a name sticker to her forehead that said: Single. Maybe even a little lonely. She hadn't felt that way in Philly, but being back in her hometown, surrounded by family and friends every day, only cast a light on how quiet her days in the city were.

"I get it. When Daisy's with friends and I'm not at the station, I'm usually at my mother's dinner table." Nick gave a bashful smile that might have made her fall in love with him all over again if she lost her senses.

"One of the perks of being back in your hometown," Carly said, smiling easier. She looked over to see Nana standing on the patio, half inside the door. Her face lit up when she saw Nick.

"Ah, Nick. You've arrived."

"And I come bearing libations," Nick said as they approached.

From behind his broad shoulders, Carly raised her eyebrows at her grandmother, who purposefully refused to make eye contact.

"Jill and Becca should be here any moment. Why don't you two enjoy that wine while I finish getting everything ready? There should be a bottle opener already on the table."

Carly could only shake off a smile when her grandmother slipped back into the house. Somewhere between going to pick flowers and now, two wine glasses and a corkscrew had appeared on the table. Miraculous!

She set the flowers in the jug that was already filled with water and said, "Well, a glass of wine never hurt anyone." And right now, she felt nervous, prickly even. It was one thing for her grandmother to try to push her back onto Nick, but why would Nick feed into it?

Nick poured them each a glass of wine, catching Nana Parker's eager gaze through the kitchen window when he turned to set the bottle down. He hid his smile as she quickly darted from view.

Leaning across the table, he whispered, "I think your grandmother is trying to keep you in town."

"That obvious, huh?" Carly laughed, a light, soft sound that he hadn't realized how much he'd missed until now. It was a sound that defined one single, perfect summer. One where the days felt longer, extending well into the nights, and they were lulled into a sense that somehow, it was endless. Until it ended. "About as obvious as the hole she's cut in the hedge."

"Ah, so you're blaming your elderly, sweet grandmother for your spying?"

"I wasn't *spying*." Carly stopped, pinching her mouth against her smile. "What can I say, if there's a hole in the hedge, I'm going to peep through it."

"And was there anything interesting to report?" he asked, growing curious.

"Maybe," she mused, squinting her eyes. She lifted her glass. "But I'd rather be on this end of one of Nana's schemes."

He widened his eyes and watched as her cheeks flamed. "I was just about to say the same," he said before she could explain away her omission. She liked spending time with him. And he'd be lying to himself if he didn't enjoy every minute spent with her. "I can't think of a better way to spend a Saturday night."

She gave a small smile, her blush fading a little. "But you must miss Daisy on the days she's not with you."

"Those are rare, and while I do enjoy my time with her, it's important for her to have friends."

"Important for you too?" Carly asked.

"Everyone at the station has been great. We make some time for team bonding, sometimes families are included too. But as for anyone special..." He met her gaze for a long moment. "That's not easy to find, is it?"

"No," she said, her voice thick.

They both took a long sip of wine as the silence lingered,

but it was all too soon interrupted by the sound of a latch opening, and Jill and Becca appearing in the yard through the garden gate.

The back door to the house flung open and Nana hissed loudly. "I told you two to come around the front!"

Jill looked alarmed but there was no hiding the amusement in Becca's grin when she looked at Carly, who rolled her eyes.

"It's fine, Nana. We're all here. And it's supposed to be a dinner party, right?" Carly cast him a rueful glance. "This feels like déjà vu from our night at the pizza parlor."

"So I wasn't the only one who noticed that Maria seemed to be doing a lot of dusting of tables that night?"

They smiled at each other for a moment and then looked up at Jill and Becca, who now shyly made their way to the table, muttering their apologies, while Nana tsked loudly and told them she'd bring out more wine glasses.

Nick rose, about to offer to help, but Nana just shooed him away. "Please. Sit. Enjoy the company. Jill can help me," she said pertly.

Jill, who was in mid-sitting position, looked startled. Giving a weary sigh, she stood and followed her grandmother into the house.

"Poor Jill," Becca said, taking a sip of Carly's wine. "She's so tired from so many hours on her feet, but she never can stand up to Nana."

"Can anyone?" Carly said with a laugh. "But Nana and Jill are the most alike."

"Stubborn," Becca agreed in a whisper, her eyes

widening when she saw her grandmother and sister returning.

Soon, the table was filled with food, and plates and chairs were moved per Nana's instruction, and before Nick knew it, he was seated beside Carly, so close that he could smell the sweet scent of her perfume, which he happened to know from way back wasn't perfume at all. Just a day well spent in the bakery.

"Nick, are there many single men at the fire station?" Nana Parker asked as soon as the pasta had been passed around.

Nick coughed, choking a little on his wine, and then hid his smile with a gulp while he watched Becca and Jill shoot looks at their grandmother.

"Oh, a few. Frankie..." He stopped there. The last thing Nana Parker needed were suggestions. If tonight was any indication, she was determined to meddle in her grand-daughters' love lives.

Not that he particularly minded, Nick thought, stealing a glance at Carly, who seemed amused at her sisters' expense. The golden highlights in her hair were catching the last of the evening light, and there was something in her smile so relaxed and pure that he wondered if she was even aware of it herself.

"Of course, we're all busy at the moment getting things set up for the carnival next week." It was a time-honored tradition and this year, the proceeds would go to pay for another truck.

"Well, the entire town is busy getting ready for the carnival!" Nana smiled. "Of course, my part is small, but it's still one I'm looking especially forward to this year."

"What's that, Nana?" Carly asked.

"Oh, didn't I tell you, dear? I was asked to judge the carnival bake-off!"

"You're judging the bake-off?" Nick glanced at Carly, but she remained very interested in moving the food around her plate.

Nana smiled proudly. "In previous years, I always entered, but when I stepped away from the bakery, Maria was kind enough to invite me to judge this year's entries instead."

"A new chapter then," Nick said, seeing that Nana Parker looked a little pained when she talked about the bakery. He knew how much it meant to her. Every memory he had of the woman was of her in an apron, usually smeared with evidence of hard work, her eyes always bright, even if sometimes her smile seemed tired.

"I'm just happy that I have granddaughters willing to carry on the legacy for as long as the town will let them," she said, smiling at the older two Sunrise Sisters before realizing her error. "And Carly, of course. She's spent more time in that bakery this past week than with me!"

Carly and her sisters exchanged glances across the table. Nick sipped his wine. And even though Nana Parker was smiling, there was a shadow over her eyes that didn't go unnoticed.

That bakery was more than just a place that sold cakes and cookies. Everyone in town had a special memory that involved it—his own being maybe a little more personal than some others. But how many people celebrated their first birthday with one of Nana's cakes? Or sat at the window with a giant brownie after a bad day, walking in with spirits low, leaving feeling at least a little brighter? He knew how much it had once meant to this town.

There had to be a way to keep Sunrise Bakery thriving, even without Nana Parker at the helm. Carly was the key to its success. Even if she didn't know it yet.

twelve

Mondays tended to be slow at Sunrise Bakery, even though Carly always thought it was the one morning of the week when people could use a pick-me-up the most.

She certainly could. A week from today, she'd be back in the sleek glass office space that housed the only place she'd ever worked—other than the bakery. Her boss would be expecting something sensational, and as of right now, Carly had absolutely nothing to show for her time in Hope Hollow, other than a thickening waistband, a strained relationship with her oldest sister, and a revived crush on Nick Sutton.

That's all it was, she told herself, as she carried a tray of peanut butter brownies into the front room, pleased to see that the new arrangement of tables was working and that most were filled.

Nick was handsome and always had been. There was no arguing with that fact any more than denying that that's all he could ever be to her. A handsome man, best admired from a distance.

Easier forgotten from a couple of hundred miles away.

Definitely not from only a few feet.

Her mouth went dry and she nearly dropped the tray when she saw him standing at the counter, hands deep in his pockets, eyes on the items in the bakery case. For a moment she thought he hadn't seen her yet and she could just slip back through the door into the kitchen and send Becca out in her place.

But then he looked up, giving her a slow grin that told her he'd known she was standing there all along, and darn it if her heart didn't immediately start to race.

"You're becoming a regular," she remarked, setting down the tray.

"I see you took my suggestion for the tables." He sounded pleased.

"More like Jill accepted the idea. It wasn't easy convincing her," she added. "But it seems to be working out."

"It's a good start," Nick said.

"Start?" Carly didn't like the sound of that. "Did you come here with more ideas?"

"I came to see if you were free tonight," Nick said bluntly.

Carly could feel the color deepen in her cheeks as heat spread down her body. She must not have hidden it well, because Nick immediately shifted on his feet and said, "For research."

Oh. Like a bucket of ice had been thrown over her, Carly felt her body temperature fade to normal.

"And what did you have in mind?" Research was part of her job. Even this trip was classified as that. Yes, she could do research.

Really, what had she been hoping for? Another shared bottle of wine at Concetti's Pizzeria?

She began messily transferring the brownies to a basket, then, realizing she was making a sloppy task of it, took a few deep breaths and started over.

"I thought we could drive to some of the neighboring towns. Check out the competition."

"Oh." She looked up at him. "Well, you know Sunrise Bakery has always catered to the locals."

He nodded. "But the locals haven't been so loyal since your grandmother retired, if I'm understanding correctly."

"She's the heart of this place. A lot of people came in just to see her every day."

"And now we have to give them a new reason to come in," he said. "Her recipes are not enough anymore."

It was a cold, harsh fact, but sometimes the truth hurt, and she knew that better than anyone.

"Okay. I'll be done here when we close up," she said, unable to stop herself from thinking of the many times she'd said those very words to the younger version of him, anticipating an evening well spent with the only person she wanted to spend it with.

"Perfect. Daisy and I will pick you up then," Nick said, backing away to let another customer step forward.

Daisy and Nick, Carly thought with a shake of her head.

As much as she was fond of that little girl, she certainly had every reminder she needed that tonight was anything but a date.

Carly didn't stand outside the bakery when the shop closed for the day. And she didn't walk down the street and stand in front of the pizza parlor either. Instead, she cut a glance across the street to the flower shop, hoping that Debbie was otherwise occupied with a pressing order and that the local phone chain wouldn't catch wind of her getting into the car with Nick and his daughter.

Instead, she started to make her way toward the bookstore, the safest place in town for her purposes, but then realized that she didn't even know what Nick's car looked like.

With a sigh, she turned around, realizing she'd probably drawn more attention to herself by walking up and down Main Street in the early evening hours, and parked herself on a bench under the shade of a maple tree.

It didn't take long for a black SUV to pull up in front and for Daisy's head to poke out of the backseat window. "We're going on a research trip!"

A research trip. Again, like she needed any sobering. Work. Not personal. Certainly not a date.

Carly darted her eyes back to the bakery, even though she knew that Jill was prepping in the kitchen and that Becca was taking the day's leftovers over to the hospital on the edge of town.

Fighting back a flutter of nerves, she walked over to the car, opened the door, and locked eyes with Nick.

"Hey," she said, her voice catching in her throat at the sight of that dark gaze.

He gave a little smile. "Hey."

It was silly, perhaps, to waver at sliding into the car beside him. Once, it had been so natural. A daily occurrence that one summer they'd shared, sometimes starting out early in the mornings, other times when she was finally able to hang her apron at the bakery. Nana had approved of Nick, and she probably had all her friends in town keeping an eye on things too, no doubt. There was no curfew for those dates, but they were responsible, getting home by ten, especially when Carly had to be up before dawn to help her family in the bakery.

"Sorry," she said, realizing that she'd hesitated long enough for a little frown to appear between his eyebrows. "I was wondering what happened to the Jeep."

Now he grinned wider and waited for her to close the door after her before saying, "I haven't thought of that old car in ages!"

"It was a great car," Carly said with a wistful sigh.

"It was." Nick gave a firm nod, his eyes on the road as he merged with traffic. "I have a lot of great memories of that car."

He glanced at her and she blushed, looking away, out the window, wondering if he was remembering the way they used to kiss right there in the front seat long after he'd pulled to a stop in Nana's driveway.

"What kind of memories?" Daisy chirped from the backseat.

Now it was Nick who flashed her a look of panic and she knew at once that he had been thinking of the exact same moments as she had.

Carly craned her neck to face the little girl. "Oh...just singing to the radio. Driving out to the lake."

Daisy grinned. "My dad still does that. With me. In this car!"

Carly raised an eyebrow at Nick, who briefly caught it. "What can I say? Not much about me has changed."

No, not much had, Carly thought. On the surface, maybe. He was driving a big, safe vehicle with a daughter strapped into the backseat. But he was still the same Nick who liked to roll down the windows and turn up the radio.

The same Nick who would kiss her until Nana would fling open the door and come out in her terrycloth robe, looking only slightly annoyed by the headlights interrupting her night's slumber.

"So," Carly said. "What's our first stop?"

"I thought we'd try the closest competitor," Nick said.

"Mapleton Bakery?" Carly pulled up an image of the tired bakery in the neighboring town that she'd only passed by a few times on her way to the bigger shopping mall.

"Actually, they got put out of business years ago," Nick said. "There's a new one now. Some little place that Daisy said her friends like to go to for their birthdays."

That didn't sound good. "Okay, then."

They arrived in what felt like no time, which only added to

the sense of unease that Carly felt. The town of Mapleton had grown since she'd been back; unlike Hope Hollow, there were national brand-name retailers lining the Main Street, and most of the shops and restaurants seemed higher-end. It wasn't surprising that there was a lot of activity on the sidewalks.

But the more concerning image was that of the bakery itself. Its storefront was painted a cheerful and eye-catching pink, and the window display was bright and playful. Out front, there were several bistro tables, filled of course, and it didn't take a fortune teller to know just how cute it would be inside.

"You've got to be kidding me," Carly muttered under her breath when they walked inside a few minutes later.

The room was set up how Sunrise now was—with a wall of benches and tables, and smaller tables in clusters throughout the room. And every seat was occupied. Only unlike Sunrise with its mismatched chairs and tables, the tables here were a crisp white, and the chairs were brightly painted in pastel colors.

"They have a garden out back, too," Daisy said excitedly. "And princess cakes. And unicorn cakes. And confetti cakes!"

And basically, every other colorful confection that Carly could think of or even name. She walked up to the display case as the line inched forward, thinking of how modern the offerings were in comparison to the more traditional recipes they offered at Sunrise.

Nick did the ordering. A slice of cake, two different kinds of cookies, a brownie, and today's special, which turned out to be strawberry pie.

No one made a strawberry pie like Nana, of this Carly was sure.

Feeling a little more confident, they found a table as a family was finishing up.

"Here, honey, let the next family sit down," the mother said to her little boy, as she collected their empty plates and napkins.

"Oh." Carly glanced at Nick, but he either hadn't heard the comment or didn't intend to correct it.

Flushed, Carly thanked the woman and sat down. Daisy already started in on the cake. "This is delicious!" she exclaimed, smiling through a bite.

Carly would be the judge of that. She picked up a fork and took a bite, realizing instantly that Daisy was right. It was delicious. The sponge was light and perfectly sweet, and the frosting was smooth with a hint of raspberry. It wasn't just beautiful to look at: it was a pleasure to eat.

They moved on to the cookies next—oversized, one a basic chocolate chip and the other an iced sugar cookie.

"The sugar cookie is better than what we have at Sunrise," Carly admitted, feeling disloyal to her grandmother, whose heart would be broken to hear her granddaughter ever admit such a thing. She took another bite, trying to cite the difference. A touch more sugar perhaps. A little less baking time to give it that extra softness. A splash of more vanilla.

"But the iced cookies aren't as good as your unicorn cookies," Daisy said firmly.

"She's right," Nick said. He held out a piece and, reluctantly, Carly took it.

They were right. And she didn't just think this out of pride, either. Her recipe had been better. But then, she'd experimented with it over the years, tweaking the measurements until it was just the way she liked it.

She just hadn't expected others to feel the same way.

"I'm not sure I even want to try the brownie," she said with a sigh. "I already know where it stands." She frowned at Nick.

"What about the pie?" he asked.

Carly stared at it for a moment, not sure if she was willing to push her luck.

"You be the judge," she said.

Nick picked up his fork and took a big bite, his expression giving nothing away. Carly knew that strawberry pie had been his favorite, and it had been her favorite to make because of that. And she just wasn't sure she could bear to think that he preferred someone else's strawberry pie to hers.

That he could prefer someone else to her.

"The pie has nothing on Sunrise Bakery," he said firmly.

Suspicious, Carly squinted her eyes and forked off a bite, relieved to see that this was true, he wasn't just being kind, not that she would have minded if that had been the case. Not entirely.

"So we're still winning in the pie department." She was relieved by the small victory. All hope wasn't lost yet.

"See? You know what's working," Nick pointed out.

"But I'm not sure this is really a direct competitor. Sure, it's close, and it's a bakery, but look around. Everyone here is young. Young mothers with their children."

"The next generation," Nick said matter-of-factly.

And there it was. He'd found the problem so quickly that Carly hadn't been able to see it, even when she wasn't as close to things as her sisters or Nana.

People came to Sunrise Bakery to see Nana. And now that Nana wasn't there anymore, it was up to the next generation. But they weren't pulling in the older generation who was there for more than a Danish. And they weren't pulling in the new generation who were looking for something different than Nana's tried and true recipes.

"I think I understand," she said sadly.

"What do you say we go have a real dinner now?" Nick said, collecting the remainder of the brownie before Daisy went into a sugar coma. He glanced at Carly. "There's a pizza place down the street. Dare we risk word getting back to Maria?"

Carly laughed, and even though she could think of an easy excuse to get back to the house, she knew that Nana would rather her be out with Nick.

"That sounds like just what I need," she said with a smile.

She caught his eye across the table, feeling her heart turn over. And it was just what she wanted too.

~

The pizza place had nothing on Concetti's, which seemed to make all of them happy.

"Frankie and Maria will be proud to hear it," Carly said as they finished their slices. She thought of something when he came to mind. "Did you ever think of being a volunteer firefighter like Frankie?"

Nick set a few bills on the table as they stood, seeming to consider the question but not for the first time.

"I did. But then it just seemed like more hours spent working." He paused while they walked out the door and toward the car, Daisy skipping ahead. "My dad was always on call at the hospital growing up and hard work was in my blood from an early age."

Carly grinned. "It's funny how things like that get passed down through the generations."

"But what I was doing in Boston wasn't the same as saving lives," he said, slanting her a glance as they approached the car. "And it had the same toll on Daisy. She…didn't seem happy in Boston. I couldn't justify that when I moved back here."

"You're wrong about one thing, though," Carly told him after they'd settled into the car. "I'm sure that you did make a difference to all those businesses you helped. I know you've made a difference with the bakery."

The sincerity in his eyes reminded her of the way he'd always been able to make her feel less alone in this world. "I hope so. And to be honest…it's been kind of fun."

She glanced at him as he focused on the road, wondering if he was talking about the work or something else. Something like spending time with her. Because despite the circumstances, she had to admit that she was enjoying herself too.

~

"You want to come back for a nightcap?" Nick asked when they crossed the town line into Hope Hollow.

He sensed Carly hesitate before she nodded, then said, "Don't you have to get Daisy to bed?"

He glanced up in the rearview mirror to see Daisy asleep in the backseat even though it wasn't late.

"Sugar crash," he declared. "She'll be out for the night."

"Well, sugar for dinner will do that to you," Carly said, laughing lightly.

"You must think I'm a pretty crappy father," Nick said, half-teasing.

But when Carly spoke, there was no joking in her tone. "I think that you're a wonderful father, Nick."

Some days, he knew he was a good dad. Other times, it helped to hear it. But coming from Carly? It meant a lot. It meant that he'd made the right choice.

"As much as I'd love to come over, I don't have a way of getting home, and something tells me that Daisy isn't old enough to stay home by herself."

"And here I thought I was detail-oriented," he joked, covering his embarrassment. He'd gotten swept up in the day, the way he always did with time with Carly. He'd stopped thinking about practical matters until they were right there, and he had no choice but to accept them.

"Bakery then?" he asked.

She glanced at him. "Actually, I walked to the bakery this morning. So, looks like you'll be dropping me off at home."

He felt a slow grin tug at his mouth. "Does your grand-mother know where you were this evening?"

"No!" Carly exclaimed and then dropped her voice to a

whisper. "If she knew I had enjoyed a slice of cake at another bakery, I think she'd probably change the locks."

"I meant," Nick said archly, "did she know that you were with me?"

"Oh." Carly fought off a grin. "No. And I expect that when she sees the car in her driveway, she'll be hiding behind the curtains of the dining room, speed dialing your mother."

Nick barked out a laugh as he pulled onto her street. It was a familiar drive, one he'd made so many times, one that brought him back to a happier time in his life when everything felt possible.

"Looks like there's one way to find out."

He braked in the driveway and shifted the gear into park, knowing his headlights were shining brightly enough to rouse suspicion from Nana, who couldn't possibly be asleep this early.

"Well," Carly said, smiling over at him. "Thank you. This was...enlightening."

That was one word for it. Only he wasn't thinking about baked goods right now. His gaze drifted over Carly's pretty face, down to her full, pink mouth, and he felt a pull that wasn't easy to resist, one that felt so natural, so right. Once, so easy.

Before he could lean in farther, Carly released her seat belt and reached for the door.

"This was nice, Nick," she said, her smile seeming tighter.

He gave a resigned grin, nodding as he pressed back into his seat. He watched as Carly walked up the driveway and cut across the path toward the front door, where Nana Parker's image had appeared behind a rustling of curtains in the dining room, wondering if she felt the same sense of lost opportunity that he did.

Then he glanced up at the rearview mirror again and told himself that as disappointing as the night had ended, it had probably been for the best. He had Daisy to think about now.

And the last thing he ever wanted to do was let her down. Or have her start missing Carly the way he knew he would. And already did.

thirteen

Carly walked into the kitchen the next morning with fresh eyes. Jill was putting a lattice topping on a strawberry pie and Becca was stirring a batter for what Carly knew were the blueberry streusel muffins.

The very muffins that tended to be given out as leftovers most evenings.

"What can I get started on?" she asked as she tied her apron strings.

Becca didn't stop stirring. "Oh, maybe the chocolate chip scones?"

Carly did as she was told and took a mixing bowl down from the shelf and then stopped. "What if we try a new special today?" she suggested.

Now, both of her sisters stopped what they were doing to stare at her.

Swallowing hard, Carly continued. "I could make some raspberry bars. They're a big hit with my coworkers. Or—"

"People will be expecting the scones," Jill said, going back to her task.

"And the muffins," Becca added.

Carly felt her shoulders deflate but she wasn't willing to let it go just yet. "But wouldn't it be nice to give them some new options? Something...unexpected?"

Becca winced a little and then shrugged. "I don't know, Carly. Sunrise has been serving Nana's recipes since long before we were born. That's what we're known for. That's what's kept us going."

"Only it's not keeping us going anymore," Carly said gently.

A silence fell over the room and for a moment Carly dared to think that her sisters were receptive to the idea of changing things up around here.

"Nana entrusted us with her recipes," Jill said, shaking her head. "We promised to honor that."

"I know." Carly felt defeated as she reached for the flour and began measuring it out. "And that's what makes Sunrise Bakery so special. It's why I wanted to feature it in the magazine."

"What do you mean?" Jill looked up at her, her eyes alert.

Carly sighed and explained the article she'd planned to write. "It was going to showcase how special a small business can be. How a family can pass it along, through the generations."

Jill's mouth slacked. "But you walked away from the bakery a long time ago, Carly."

"I'm still a part of this family, and this is a family business. And...this was my way of still being a part of it."

Becca gave her a sad smile. "You're always a part of this family, Carly. You always were. This bakery is just part of that family."

"A central part, though," Carly emphasized. She sighed. "Now, though, I'm not sure I can really write anything if the bakery might be closed by the time the article comes out. If it even ever came out. My editor invited three of us to write a feature story, but only one will make the cut."

"Oh, I see, so you were just using the bakery to advance your career?" Jill set her hands on her hips, leaving flour marks on her apron.

"It's not like that—" Carly insisted, except that maybe it was. When she'd pitched the idea to her editor, she hadn't been thinking of the family business at all, had she? She'd been thinking of a bigger title. A bigger paycheck. A bigger apartment. A promotion that only one assistant would earn.

Things that she thought could bring her more happiness, fill some sense of emptiness that had been lingering for so long, she'd learned to live with it.

Until she'd come back here.

"I don't want to lose the bakery," she said firmly. "Not just because of the article. Because being here has made me remember all the good times we had, and not just us, but Nana. And...Mom."

A silence fell over the room. They'd all dealt with the loss of their mother in their own ways, and they didn't discuss it often.

"I know how hard you took the loss," Becca said gently.

Carly swallowed hard and willed herself not to cry but her hands were shaking when she reached for the sugar canister. She looked at Jill. "I never gave up on this bakery, Jill. Right now, it feels like you're the one who's giving up on it."

"Me?" Jill shook her head. "I'm the one who's been here every day from before dawn to dusk. I'm the one who stayed behind. You didn't see me going off to the big city for college or some fancy job. I was right here. Protecting our family recipes. Guarding our family legacy. If anyone gave up on this bakery, it was you, Carly."

"That's not fair," Carly said, her voice rising a notch. "The two of you always had a connection with this place that I didn't share. But I'm older now; I appreciate it more."

"It's always easy to look back and realize how great something was once it's gone," Jill said, but the edge was fading from her tone. She leaned against the counter, her eyes full of sadness when they met Carly's. "I tried. Becca tried."

"Then let me try!"

"Carly, you're leaving town on Sunday. Do you really think you can do what we haven't been able to do in just a matter of days?"

Carly shook her head. She'd never go so far as to be that full of herself, and Jill knew it as well as Becca.

"Nick has had a few ideas..."

"Nick?" Now Becca couldn't help but smile, but she sobered herself when she caught a warning glance from Carly.

The last thing Carly wanted to do right now was to talk about something she didn't understand herself. Last night had been...nice. Really nice. But as Jill had just pointed out, she was leaving in just a few days. And that was what had stopped her from kissing Nick.

Even though she'd been kicking herself ever since she stepped out of his car.

"The chairs and tables were one thing," Jill said.

"Although it has helped," Becca pointed out. She turned her attention back to Carly. "What else does he suggest?"

Carly could feel Jill's eyes boring through her while she remained fixed on her middle sister, whose open expression showed that she was willing to at least hear some suggestions.

Ones that Jill would no doubt shoot down.

"There's a new bakery over in Mapleton," Carly began.

"Yeah, we're aware." Jill continued baking, partially because she didn't want to listen but more because there was still work to be done.

Carly measured out the sugar while she talked. "It's a big hit with the kids in Daisy's school and, well, it's a big hit in general. It's cute. It's fresh. And...it's delicious."

"And you don't think that Nana's recipes are delicious?" Jill looked at her, aghast.

"Of course I do!" Carly hesitated. "And their pie has nothing on ours. But I just think that it might help if we freshened things up a bit. You have to admit that this place hasn't changed in three generations."

"I don't know, Carly," Becca said, grimacing. "Change is risky. What if it doesn't work? We'll lose the few remaining customers we have left."

"You're already about to lose the business!"

"We can't do that to Nana. This is her business. Her life's work. And it's more than that." Jill looked pained. "It's her whole heart, this place."

Carly grew silent. "We won't know unless we try."

"It's bad enough to lose the bakery, but if we change everything and still lose it?" Jill looked at Becca, who nodded in agreement.

"It would be the worst thing we could do," she said.

Carly fell silent. Her sisters had made their decision, and once again, she was expected to just accept it or move on.

Only this time she wasn't so certain that she could do either.

Carly planted herself in her bedroom that night and began scribbling notes for the article. She was out of inspiration, and only one word came to mind: stubborn. That's what her sisters were.

That's what her grandmother was.

And maybe, that's what she'd been too. Stubborn to stay away from Hope Hollow for so long out of fear of what would happen if she ever returned. Now she was back, and in many ways, it was worse than she could have imagined.

And better too, she thought, smiling when she thought of Nick.

There was always one way to relax her mind, and with that, Carly closed her laptop, set aside her notebook, and crept down the stairs.

Nana could sleep through the worst thunderstorm—she always said she had to sleep deep given how precious little of it she got. But in all the years that Carly had lived with her, Nana had never once slept through her alarm. Usually, she woke before it went off.

She was programmed, she liked to say. And Carly was too.

All the recipes that she'd grown up with came back to her like she'd never stopped practicing them, even though in recent years she'd done just that. Her contributions to office potlucks or birthday celebrations were of her own doing, tweaked recipes that she saw in magazines or cookbooks, which she always seemed to receive as gifts in the Secret Santa exchange.

She put the kettle on for some tea and pulled a mixing bowl from the baker's rack where her grandmother kept her collection, nearly dropping it when she saw Nana standing in the entryway, tightening the belt on her robe.

"I didn't wake you, did I?" Carly felt guilty when she glanced at the clock and saw it was already nearly eleven.

"Nonsense. I can sleep when I'm dead." Nana brushed away her concern and walked deeper into the kitchen to fetch herself a mug from the cupboard beside the sink. She gave Carly the once over and said, "Something troubling you, dear?"

Carly gave a smile. "What gave it away?"

"Besides the hour?" Nana arched an eyebrow. "The mixing bowl."

Carly sighed and set it on the counter.

"I used to do that, you know. Bake when I had a problem I needed to work through, or just when...my heart was heavy." Nana frowned for a moment and Carly wondered if she was thinking about her husband or her daughter or both.

"It must be difficult not to do what you love anymore, Nana," Carly said gently.

"Who says I don't still do it?" Nana snorted. "And just because I'm not at the bakery every day doesn't mean it isn't still a part of me. It always will be, even if the doors eventually close and the sign comes down."

The kettle started to whistle and Carly flicked off the knob and then poured them each a cup of hot water. Nana reached for the canister of tea bags and dropped one in each of their mugs.

"You're not as upset as I'd expect," Carly hedged.

Nana gave a little shrug. "I've had to adapt to a lot of changes in my life. A lot of loss too. But life goes on, maybe not in the way I would have planned or wanted, but it does. And good things still happen."

Carly nodded slowly. "But the bakery, Nana."

"I've had time to accept it. Stepping away from working there was a long and difficult decision. And what's going on now didn't exactly happen overnight either."

"But won't you miss it?"

"I already do." Nana's smile was sad as she leaned into the counter. "But just because you don't see someone or something every day, that doesn't mean that they're gone. There are always the memories, so long as you hold on to them."

Carly looked down at her mug, falling silent. She'd done just that, hadn't she? Tried to run from her memories instead of holding on to them, telling herself it was easier that way, less painful.

But she wasn't ready to lose them again. And if she didn't have to, she wasn't willing to lose anything more. Not yet.

"Well, I think I'll take my tea upstairs and finish reading a book that Joanna recommended," Nana said, giving Carly a pat on the shoulder as she walked past her. "Don't stay up too late, dear."

"I won't," Carly promised, even though they both knew that the bakery was closed tomorrow.

Nana turned before she entered the hallway. "Tomorrow a bunch of people are gathering in the town square to help set up the carnival. Why don't you join me on your day off? Unless..."

"Unless?" Carly gave her grandmother a knowing look, waiting for it. Really, she was surprised that the topic hadn't come up over dinner earlier.

"I did see Nick drop you off last night," Nana said suggestively.

"Yes, but unlike in the past, there was no kiss at the end of the night," Carly pointed out. Except there almost had been. Not that she'd be making her grandmother aware of that.

Her heart began to race when she thought of the way she and Nick had left things. How he'd leaned over, their eyes locked, and for a moment, she'd dared to think—

She realized that her grandmother was still staring at her with obvious interest and she rolled her eyes skyward.

"I'd be happy to help with the carnival," she said. "I have absolutely nothing else to do tomorrow."

Other than try to think of a way to save the bakery. And maybe get a few words written down for her article.

Alone in the kitchen once more, Carly went to work on one of her personal favorite recipes, one that always won her praise every Christmas at the office holiday lunch. It was a twist on a classic shortbread cookie, and one that she and her mother had always enjoyed more than anyone else in their family. Only this one she pressed into a tart tin to create a crust that she would bake and then later fill with chocolate ganache.

When she baked in her apartment in Philly, she was alone, usually with only the television for company. But here, she knew her grandmother was upstairs, sipping her tea, and right here in this very kitchen, at these very chairs, she'd spent some of the happiest moments of her life.

By the time she'd turned out the light, she'd nearly convinced herself to take Nick's lead and enter the contest. If only to show her sisters that she too could be a contributing member of the so-called family bakery.

fourteen

Like usual, Nana insisted on walking into town the next morning, and as they passed Frannie's house, Carly thought about what she'd seen the other day. She decided not to mention it, though, when she saw the pinch of her grandmother's lips as they walked by. Frannie and Nana had never been close after that incident with the welcome basket, but enemy status had been established when one of Frannie's baked goods beat Nana's in the Spring Carnival bake-off eighteen years ago. Carly had only been ten, but she could still remember the look of horror on Nana's face when she was awarded the red ribbon instead of the blue.

After that, she'd made it a point never to lose again. Now, Carly wondered if Nana could be an unbiased judge should Frannie decide to enter this year.

And then Carly thought about Nick's suggestion for her entry—and what that would mean if she won.

Or if she didn't.

She was happy when they reached the town square

where a large crowd had gathered on this sunny day, broken out into groups to handle the various tasks.

"Isn't that Mr. Quincy?" Carly gestured to the man whose smile was obvious even from half a football field's length.

"Pshaw." Nana pursed her lips and flicked her gaze around the square. "I'll look for Debbie or Maria."

Carly fought back her amusement as she watched Nana hurry across the lawn, Mr. Quincy watching her the entire time.

With a sigh, she turned and looked around for any sign of Joanna or even one of her sisters, but her heart skipped a beat when she saw Nick standing with a group of guys from the fire station, setting up the staging area for the band.

She walked over slowly, feeling the eyes of half the town on her back, and gave him a wave from a safe distance.

He grinned, said something to Frankie, laughed with a shake of his head, and then joined her. She waited, watching as he approached. His long strides closed the distance quickly.

"I didn't expect to see you here today." His gaze held hers. "Not that I'm complaining."

She was sure that half the town was watching this exchange, including her grandmother, but the only person she could think about right now was the man standing in front of her in jeans and a tee shirt that his chest filled out quite nicely.

"Well, I'm still a member of this town," she said. At least for a few more days.

"I thought you'd be hard at work on that article on your day off from the bakery."

"Still waiting for inspiration," she said. "Maybe I'll find some today."

Her mouth quirked because she suspected the only inspiration she'd have today would be coming straight from Nick and the power he still held over her when he smiled at her like that.

"You'll at least find a distraction," he said. His gaze lingered on hers for a moment and she wondered if he was replaying the other night like she was, how close they had been to taking a step forward, or maybe, a step back.

Did he regret that they hadn't kissed? Or, like her, was he trying to remain sensible, and practical? Because they'd never been reckless, never followed their hearts. They'd done the rational thing ten years ago. They could certainly do the same now.

She cleared her throat. "So...what should I get started on?"

"Daisy's working on some signs." He caught the surprise in her expression and explained, "She said she had a stomachache yesterday so she stayed home from school an extra day to be on the safe side. Between us, I think she had too many sweets on our research trip."

Carly laughed. "Would it be terrible of me to wish that it was the sweets themselves? Something that might shut the competition's doors for good?"

"Believe me, I thought the same thing, but I think it was a case of good, old-fashioned sugar overdose. And poor judgment on my part," he said, chagrined.

She elbowed him lightly as he led the way over to the picnic table where Daisy sat coloring a poster board. "You're one of the best fathers I've known. Not that I have much personal experience."

Nick didn't need an explanation. He knew that she'd never really known her own father, and how close she was to her mother as a result. "It must have been hard for you. Losing your mother so young. Now that I see it through Daisy's eyes...I can't imagine."

Only something in his tone told her that he could imagine and that the dynamic with Daisy's mother was difficult at best.

"I had my grandmother," Carly pointed out. "And my sisters. And this town."

The one she'd given up, she realized with shame, even though she hadn't done it out of malice or spite. At the time it had felt like the only way to move forward instead of being buried by the past.

"And you turned out all right." He gave her a mischievous grin and she felt her smile grow against the heaviness in her chest.

"Daisy will too. She has you. Your parents. This entire community."

They both stopped to stare at Daisy from the distance, sharing a smile, both probably thinking of how much different Nick's life would have been if he'd made a different choice. How much different Daisy's would have been.

How much worse.

"It wasn't an easy decision," he said, turning to look her in the eye. "All those years ago."

She swallowed hard, pushing back the building emotions that carried her right back to that awful day when instead of greeting her with his usual grin, he wore a frown that told her everything was about to change.

She'd seen frowns like that before. She was no stranger to what came next.

"I know," she whispered. Then, braving a smile, she said, "But it was the right one, Nick." She set a hand on his arm, the connection so easy and yet so foreign at the same time, nearly as intimate as a kiss after all this time, then dropped her hand just as quickly.

"You seem pretty happy with your life in Philly." He said, but there was a question in his eye.

She stared at him, thinking of just how unfulfilling that life was. How empty. How routine. How without that promotion it lacked any direction, and even with it—it now seemed to lack purpose.

But Nick needed to hear that she was okay. That she had done just fine on the path she'd chosen when he'd left her no other real choice at all.

"I am," she said, giving a firm nod.

Nick's phone rang and he gave her a grimace of apology, but his expression turned more serious when he glanced at the screen.

"Sorry, I need to take this."

Carly nodded. "Of course." But as she watched the expression on Nick's face turn to a deeper frown, she couldn't help but wonder what could be troubling him so much.

She walked away, toward the table where Daisy was

working on her poster. "What do you say we get out the glitter?" she suggested.

Daisy's brown eyes lit up. "Yeah!"

With Daisy momentarily distracted, Carly cut a glance over to where Nick was standing, his defensive stance making her wonder who he could be talking to, and what could be troubling him.

"Carly? Can you help with the glue?"

Carly forced her attention back to Daisy. "Of course. I happen to be an expert with glue."

"I think you're an expert at lots of things."

"Oh?" Carly smiled, amused.

"You bake the best cookies. And you work at the bakery, so you probably bake cakes and pies, too. And you have pretty hair," Daisy added.

"Why thank you!" Carly knew the compliment was coming from a nine-year-old, but she couldn't help but feel flattered enough to touch her ponytail.

"And you make my dad really happy."

Now Carly felt her smile slip. She swallowed hard, unsure of how to respond to that, but Daisy was already carefully shaking the glitter onto the pattern that Carly had made with the glue, her little mouth pinched in concentration.

By the time Nick rejoined them a few minutes later, she had already covered most of the posterboard, and her hands, with the glitter.

"Look, Daddy! Isn't it pretty? Carly helped me."

"It's beautiful, honey. But why don't you go over to the bathroom and wash your hands?" He gestured to her sticky fingers, which were leaving glittery fingerprints on everything she touched, which so far was only the posterboard and the plastic table covering.

Carly watched as she scampered away and then she turned to Nick as he took his seat.

"Everything okay?"

Nick glanced over his shoulder to make sure that Daisy was out of earshot.

"That was Daisy's mother," he explained.

"Ah." Now Carly wished she hadn't asked, but the look on Nick's face told her that he had a lot on his mind. "Call didn't go well?"

"Every call with Daisy's mother has been frustrating lately. She loves Daisy, I know she does, but she doesn't realize how hard Daisy takes it every time she breaks plans."

"That must be hard." Carly could tell from the lines on Nick's forehead that it wasn't just tough on his daughter.

"I can only protect her so much." Nick sighed heavily. "If I had it my way, Daisy's life would be settled, secure, and stable."

"It is settled, secure, and stable," Carly assured him, leaning in across the table. She set her hand on his, giving it a squeeze. "Look at her. She's having a great time, everyone in this town knows her and looks out for her. And she's got the best dad. She even told me so."

Nick barked out a laugh, and she could see the worry leaving his shoulders.

She hadn't even realized she was still holding his hand until she looked down. His skin was smooth and warm under her palm, and oh so familiar. With a start, she snatched her hand back, setting it safely in her lap where it belonged.

"You can't shield her from every disappointment in life," she told Nick softly. "As much as you want to, there are some things that you won't be able to control. Just keep doing the best you can. That's what matters to kids."

"When did you get to be so wise?" he asked, a slow grin lifting the corners of his mouth.

He was looking at her so intensely, his eyes so warm, the pull so strong, that Carly struggled to look away, even though a part of her really wanted to.

The other part of her wanted to stay in this moment. Maybe, to never let it end.

"Oh, somewhere between the last time you saw me and today, I suppose. Life is a strange road. We can't always plan for what comes next." Or count on it, she thought, tearing her gaze from his.

"I suppose that's what keeps things interesting," he said.

"You seem to be feeling a little better," she said, giving him a raise of an eyebrow.

"How can I not when I'm in such good company?" He grinned, but then, perhaps seeing her blush, cleared his throat. "Well, I suppose I should lasso my daughter in case she wanders off."

Carly laughed, feeling more relaxed. "And where would she wander to? Seems to me she has everything she needs right here in this town square."

He looked at her again. "We both do."

Right. Now Carly thought it would be a good time to make sure that Daisy hadn't found trouble, even though she highly doubted that there was any to be found here in this sleepy little town.

They stood, and Carly left the poster on the table to dry. Across the green, there were squeals and laughter, and it didn't take long to find Daisy playing on the swings with some other girls.

"Yep, everything she needs right here in this square." Nick looked content when he watched his daughter from a distance. "I guess I worry too much."

"Isn't that what all parents do?" Then, catching his knowing look, she realized she'd misspoken. Clearly, Daisy's mother didn't worry—but then, with Nick being such a hands-on parent, maybe she didn't need to.

"So how long does this setup last?" she asked, shifting onto safer topics.

Nick turned and gave her an affronted look, but the gleam in his eyes told her he was joking. "Are you that eager to get away? More important things to do? Better places to be?"

"Not eager," she corrected. "But I do have some things to do. And as for better places to be..." She shook her head and looked around the square, lined with trees and bursting with flowers blooming in shades of pink and purple. The gazebo sat in the center, reminding her of the first kiss that she and Nick had ever shared, on a rainy day, when they'd had to dart across the lawn for shelter.

She felt the pull of his stare, watching her, and she wondered if he remembered that day. She wondered if he felt anything when he looked at that gazebo.

Then she told herself that she was being ridiculous. Nick

was desensitized to those memories by now, surely. He faced them every day.

And he'd filled his life with plenty of new moments since then.

She, on the other hand, didn't have much to show for things other than a shaky career and a cramped apartment with fickle heating.

"I'm still working on my article, and I'm afraid that I haven't put in as much time as I should."

"Too busy having fun?" he chided.

"Yes," she admitted. Because working at the bakery had turned out to be more enjoyable than she remembered it being. And because seeing her old friends—and flings—was more than a little distracting.

"When's it due?"

"Monday. When I'm back in the office."

Nick nodded, falling silent, and even Carly had nothing more to say. Suddenly all banter, all this confidence, seemed to feel pointless given how soon she'd be leaving again.

"But...there's something else I need to work on too," she said, feeling her pulse begin to race. He looked at her questioningly and she pulled in a breath. "I'm going to enter the bake-off. With one of my own recipes."

Nick looked at her with interest, a slow grin lifting the corner of his mouth. "What made you change your mind?"

"I guess I figure that I have nothing to lose. And...it would be easier to leave town this time if I knew that I didn't have regrets."

He gave her a long look and then stepped back when Daisy started calling out to him. And at that moment Carly knew that even if she managed to find a way to keep the bakery from closing or being sold to a national chain, even if she wrote the best article of her career and earned herself a promotion, so long as Nick was here in Hope Hollow and she wasn't, she'd always have some sense of regret, wouldn't she?

Regret. Nick was still thinking about the word long after Daisy had gone off with his mother to help with the table centerpieces for the food stands. He'd had a lot of regrets over the years, and they didn't stop with Carly. They extended to Liz, to marrying her when he wasn't in love with her, to not fighting for their marriage hard enough, or to maybe holding on to it for so long. To staying in Boston for as long as he had, where they'd been so unhappy. To coming back here, creating physical distance between his daughter and her mother even when Liz was never around anyway.

Frankie whistled at him, interrupting his thoughts, and motioned for him to help with the heavy lifting.

"Don't go dropping something on your foot," Frankie said as they picked up one of the large wooden benches and moved it across the lawn.

"Sorry. I'm just a little distracted," Nick admitted, instantly wishing he hadn't when he caught his friend's grin. It was just as mischievous as his mother's. Just as knowing, too.

"So...you and Carly have been hanging out a lot," Frankie said, shuffling backward, never losing his grip.

"Why don't you focus on your own love life instead of mine?" Nick joked.

"Ah, so you admit that there's something going on between the two of you." Frankie grinned.

Nick just shook his head. There was no point defending himself, not when what Frankie had said was partly true.

"How'd your last date go?" he asked instead, switching the focus onto Frankie's mother's endless pool of eligible women for him.

"She was great," Frankie said, surprising Nick. He came to a stop and dropped the bench to the grass. "But—"

"Don't tell me," Nick said, lowering his hold on the bench.

"She cut her spaghetti," Frankie said gravely.

Nick, who hadn't been expecting this offense, tossed his head back and laughed. "And here I thought it couldn't get much worse than the girl who already started calling your mother Mom."

"Mamma Maria," Frankie corrected, raising an eyebrow.

"To be fair, a lot of people around here call your mother that. It's a term of endearment."

"Well, even Mamma Maria couldn't be upset with me for calling it a night before dessert with this one," Frankie said, sounding discouraged. "Who cuts spaghetti? Name one person!"

Nick grimaced. "Daisy?"

"Ah, but Daisy's a kid." Frankie tossed his hand through the air but then looked at Nick sharply. "And her Uncle Frankie's going to be having a word with her about that before she's ten. If my mother doesn't get to her first."

"She already has!" Nick laughed again. "Last time we were in there."

"I thought the last time you were in there was with Carly," Frankie said, giving him a knowing look.

Caught red-handed.

"I forgot the way people talk in this town," Nick sighed.

"Easy to forget when you've been away, I suppose. But that's the thing about Hope Hollow. Once you're back, it's like you never left."

Nick stared across the lawn to where Carly was sitting at a table with her friend Joanna, working on the garland that would be wrapped around the gazebo before the weekend festivities.

It was true, wasn't it? That it was as if no time had passed. They were still two young kids with their entire lives ahead of them.

It was easy to fall back on the way things used to be. To forget that Carly had a new life—and one she loved—somewhere else.

And that, come Monday, she'd be back at her office in the city.

And he'd be right here, still missing her.

fifteen

With Nana out of the house most of Thursday morning for her monthly gardening club meeting, Carly took the day off from the bakery to focus on her contest entry. It was a big event, and not just for Nana Parker, who used to search through her trove of family recipes until she found what she knew would be a winner. She knew better than to enter something offered daily at the bakery, instead using the bake-off as a way of gauging the crowd.

Much as Carly intended to do.

After experimenting with a cookie bar that had been a hit with her boss and a spice cake she often made for the holiday potluck, she decided to keep it simple, and, recalling how much Daisy and her friends loved the unicorn cookies, she took it one step further with a spin on her raspberry lemon cupcakes.

She hid away all evidence of her work and not just because Nana was one of the judges this year. As proud as Carly was of her creation, her stomach went all funny every time she thought about what she was doing: making one of her own recipes instead of relying on the tried and true traditions that had bound her family through the generations.

And doing it without Jill's permission. Or Nana's blessing.

It was silly, she knew. She was in her late twenties and she'd been on her own for years. But even after all this time, her sisters had a way of making her feel like she was still a kid who didn't know as much as them when it came to the bakery.

And much as it bothered her, the last thing she wanted to do was upset them.

She was still anxious when she met Nick in the parking lot across the street from the town green on Friday morning. Nana had gotten an early start, as the judges were needed well before the event kicked off. Even though it was a weekday and the businesses would be open for the day, the schools were closed in support of the carnival, and most people—including her sisters—would be gathered on the town green, watching the event that kicked everything off.

"I half expected you to show up in sunglasses and a head-scarf," Nick joked when she rolled down the window.

"Don't give me ideas," she said ruefully. "I already have my bags packed and stuffed in the trunk, just in case I need to peel out of town early."

Nick laughed, but a frown worried his forehead as he crouched down, resting his elbows on the ledge of the open window. "You don't really plan on leaving, do you?"

Well, when he asked her like that, so close that she could see the fine lines that crinkled when he looked at her with those warm, dark eyes, it was impossible to think of anything that could ever make her leave Hope Hollow.

"Not today, at least." She gave him a reassuring smile. "But I'm honestly not sure what would be worse. Winning or not winning."

"This is your chance to get a little attention for the family business. Because you are part of that family," he reminded her.

"I know that, but try telling Jill that. She's always taken propriety when it comes to Sunrise. To be honest, I never felt like there was room there for me."

"Seems to me that you're just what that place needs," Nick said. "Unless Jill would be willing to hire outside the family."

Which she wasn't. Because Jill followed the traditions. Turned them into rules. Even when they worked against her.

And now Carly was about to do what she was always accused of doing. Breaking those rules.

She pulled in a shaky breath. "I guess I've come this far. May as well see it through."

"That's the spirit!" Nick's smile widened. "And did you really think I was going to let you quit now?"

The answer was no. Because Nick had always brought out the best in her. Supported her. Encouraged her. Wanted good things for her.

So as unsure as she was about this, she decided to trust his judgment.

He jutted his chin to the backseat. "The box back there?"

Carly nodded. Of course, there was never a shortage of

appropriate bakery boxes around their house, even for a dozen cupcakes.

"Handle with care," Carly warned when Nick pulled them from the floor, where she could be sure they wouldn't slide around too much.

"I'll hold this box like it's my own baby," he assured her, before closing the door with his hip and then walking away.

A strange sense of hope washed over Carly as she watched him go, even if it might be the last one.

She'd tried everything she could this week, and time had run out for her. Maybe the bakery, too.

Certainly for her article.

But as for Nick... She couldn't think about that today, not when the bake-off was going to start in only fifteen minutes.

Carly turned off the engine and marched across the town square which had come alive with music and decorations, carnival games, and face painting, and joined the gathering crowd, scanning it for her sisters, who waved her over.

Carly pushed out a nervous breath and joined them, then caught Nick's eye across the group of onlookers. The wink he tossed her made her relax—but not much.

"I'm relieved that Nana is a judge this year. It gave me an excuse not to enter," Jill said, but the tone in her voice was wistful.

Carly realized for a moment that Jill felt duty-bound, and not just because she was the oldest, the one whose name was on the business papers, and whose finances were at stake. But because she loved what she did. She cared.

Maybe most of them all.

Carly was just about to tell her sisters what she had done when the mayor walked over to the judging table and announced the tasting was beginning.

The crowd, including Carly, fell silent as the judges sampled each of the entries. Her heart began to pound when she watched her grandmother reach for her cupcake and admire the unicorn decoration with a smile.

Carly let out a shaky sigh.

"That's awfully pretty," Jill murmured. "I wonder who made that."

"I wonder..." Carly bit back her smile until she saw Nick give her a grin of support across the crowd.

She'd piqued Jill's interest, which was half the battle, but the true judging, however, was in the taste and texture. Nana had always been opinionated about cake and rightfully so. Sometimes the simplest recipes were the most difficult to perfect.

She watched on bated breath as Nana brought the cupcake to her mouth and took a bite, her expression giving nothing away as she chewed thoughtfully and then jotted some notes on her notecard. Carly would have done anything to see what Nana was writing, even though a part of her wasn't sure she even wanted to know.

She wasn't that much different from her sisters, after all. Her grandmother's approval mattered more than anything. Now, glancing at Jill, she felt herself soften towards her oldest sister. It couldn't be easy, trying to please the woman who had loved them for all of their lives and raised them for most. She'd taught them everything she knew with pride, and they'd cherished her recipes with honor.

She was relieved when Nana moved on to the next entry —a slice of pie that didn't seem to impress her if the little purse of her lips gave anything away.

Carly used the opportunity to slip away, and her sisters, like everyone else in the crowd, were more interested in the judging than her whereabouts.

Except for Nick.

"Where are you going?" he asked, catching up to her. "They're about to announce the winner."

Carly shook her head. "I think this was a bad idea."

"A bad idea? Did you see your grandmother's face when she tasted your cupcake?"

Carly hesitated. "I saw her face when she picked up my cupcake. Style is a lot different than substance."

"Come on back and see it through," Nick urged. "You've come this far. What's the worst that can happen? You don't win?"

"Actually, I'm beginning to think that the worst that can happen is that I do." Carly felt on the verge of tears.

"Come back. Daisy's waiting for us." Nick reached for her elbow. The touch of his hand, so casual, sent a shiver through her.

Carly gave him a menacing look, but she was smiling. "You know I can't say no to that little girl."

"Then we share the same plight." He laughed, and reluctantly, Carly joined him to cut back across the lawn.

The judges had finished their scoring and were now lined up, hands folded in front of them.

The mayor reviewed the paper he'd been handed and raised his eyes to the crowd. "This year's winner is…"

Carly felt her stomach clench. The entire crowd seemed to grow still. She couldn't see her sisters anymore, and she was thankful for that.

"Entry number...four!"

Carly felt herself blanch. She'd done it. She'd actually won.

She felt Nick jab her ribs. He knew better than to say anything. No, that was her responsibility. And sure enough, the crowd was starting to look around as the mayor called out, "Entry number four! Come reveal yourself and collect your prize!"

Oh, she hadn't dared to envision this part, even though of course a part of her had hoped to win. To show that there was a demand for new flavors and fresh designs.

That even her grandmother would approve.

But would she approve when Carly was revealed as the baker?

"I can't..." she whispered to Nick.

"You can." He was grinning, so wide that his eyes were gleaming, and luckily Daisy was still oblivious until the mayor held up the winning plate. "Number four! Baker of these beautiful and delicious cupcakes!"

"Those look like your cookies, don't they, Carly?" Daisy cried out.

Every face in the crowd seemed to turn and face her then, and Carly felt her cheeks flame with heat.

She felt a few people push her forward as the others parted, clearing a path for her to approach the judging tables, where Nana stood front and center, looking at Carly with complete surprise.

Carly swallowed hard and let the mayor shake her hand.

"I didn't think I'd win,'" she whispered to her grandmother, but before she could say anything more, she was being pushed over to the side, asked for a photo, the tray of cupcakes thrust in her hands while the crowd clapped.

But what this meant for the bakery she didn't know. And looking out into the crowd and seeing her sisters' shocked expressions, she didn't know what it would do for her family either.

By the time they'd reached the face-painting stand where Daisy impatiently waited in line, Carly had nearly stopped glancing over her shoulder for one of her family members.

She looked up at Nick, who seemed only pleased by the outcome, sharing none of her inner turmoil.

"Are you gloating?" she asked, tipping her head up at him. "I think you're gloating. And I'm the one that won."

"You are. And I'm not gloating because I was the one who convinced you to enter, though, let's be fair, I was."

That forced a rueful grin from her. One that she needed.

"I'm feeling a little chuffed because people like your cupcakes. The tray was cleaned within minutes."

"Yeah, and I didn't even get one," Daisy pouted.

Carly laughed. She knew better than to read too much into what Nick had said. It was a festival, there was free food, and who wouldn't want to sample all the sweets?

"I'll make you another batch before—" She started to say

before she left, but then stopped herself just in time. Time was running out—for her article, for the bakery.

And for her and Nick.

Nick met her gaze and said, "Well, how about a celebratory drink? Punch?"

"Punch would be great," Carly said. She looked uneasily across the lawn. She hadn't seen either of her sisters or her grandmother since she'd accepted the ribbon. Everything had become a blur then, and Jill and Becca had probably gone straight back to the bakery, even though business was sure to be even slower than usual today.

She knew she could find them and ask what they thought, but she wasn't ready just yet to hear what they had to say. She was too busy basking in the joy that she had won —and that more importantly several people had come up to her asking to place orders for the cupcakes for their upcoming birthday parties. Of course, she told them she'd have to let them know.

Meaning she'd have to talk to Jill first.

"Have you...seen my grandmother?" she asked Nick when he handed her the drink. Daisy abandoned her punch to play a nearby game with some girls her age, and Nick motioned to a bench where they could sit in the shade with a little privacy, too.

"No, but the whole town is here. She's probably lost in the crowd."

Carly nodded, telling herself that was probably it, even though her stomach felt a little funny. "I just hope she doesn't think I stepped on her toes."

"Are you kidding me? She's probably thrilled that you beat Frannie James," he said with a laugh.

Carly smiled at that. "You always know how to cheer me up," she said.

"I could say the same for you," Nick said. "And Daisy." He hesitated for a moment. "It's been really nice spending time together like this. I hope..."

She stared at him, her heart beginning to pound. He hoped what? The very things she hoped for? The ones she also couldn't bring herself to say out loud or even think about?

That she hoped that this moment would last longer than it could. Longer than this day, this evening, or evening this weekend. That she and Nick might look forward to tomorrow, and the next day, just as they once had.

"Mommy!" Daisy cried out, interrupting Carly's thoughts.

Carly registered the confusion on Nick's face for only a brief second, before she followed his gaze to where Daisy was now embracing a woman who looked everything and nothing like Carly had once imagined. Her blond hair was cut in a sleek bob that grazed her chin. She was tall, thin, and dressed for city life, not a small-town carnival.

Carly wondered if that was how others saw her too. As an outsider, someone who didn't fit in here.

Because that's all she could think of right now. Nick's ex-wife didn't fit in here—not at the carnival, not in this town, and not in this rosy dynamic that she, Nick, and Daisy had created these last two weeks.

Except that she did. She was Daisy's mother. Nothing could change that and nothing should.

And for the second time, Carly knew that there was nothing she could do but give Nick a little smile and say, "It's okay. I'll be fine."

"I'm sorry, Carly. I didn't know she was coming." Nick's forehead bore the anguish he carried in his voice.

"It's fine. I promised Joanna we'd go on the Ferris wheel together for old times' sake."

He looked torn. "If you're sure?"

"It's fine," she told him again. Just fine.

Even though she had the awful feeling that nothing was fine at all.

Liz wanted to leave the carnival early to spend some quiet time with Daisy, and Nick didn't argue. The town was full of people he knew. People who wanted the best for him. People who didn't think that Liz was that.

And maybe she wasn't. Maybe she never had been. But try telling that to Daisy, who didn't even care that she hadn't gotten her face painted.

Daisy took Liz straight up to her room when they got back to the house and Nick used the time to sit downstairs, to think, and to try to push the image of Carly from his mind. The disappointment that she'd tried to hide. The same that he shared and couldn't express. For not the first time.

For dinner, he made a frozen pizza, because it was easy,

and because his mind was going a hundred miles an hour. Daisy kept things busy by doing most of the talking during dinner, and later when they had ice cream for dessert.

Nick waited until Daisy was in bed to open a bottle of wine, knowing that a conversation was inevitable. He took his time pouring it, glancing up every few seconds to see Liz wandering around the living room, pausing to look at the framed photos he had set on the mantle—special moments that he'd shared with Daisy since they'd moved back to town, his favorite being one of her at the local pumpkin patch.

Pulling in a breath, he walked into the room and extended a glass.

She took it with a fleeting smile. "None of me, I see."

"There's a picture of you and Daisy on her nightstand," he replied. Then, feeling uneasy by having to explain, he said, "We're no longer together, Liz."

"And are you together with someone else? That woman you were with at the carnival?"

Nick hesitated. Whatever was going on with Carly was confusing and unclear, but Liz was perceptive, and she wasn't completely off base in this case, either. Carly might be in town temporarily but they'd reconnected, confirming the bond that he'd tried to ignore.

"I'm trying to rebuild my life," was all he said.

"And I am too," she replied.

Oh, he knew. He knew all about the life that Liz craved. One that didn't make her always wonder what might have been, what she could have had, if circumstances hadn't unfolded the way they had.

"That's actually why I'm here," she said, looking him in the eye.

He raised an eyebrow. He didn't really care about her plans, not unless they directly involved Daisy. What Liz did in her free time wasn't his business anymore. Now, though, he was curious to see what she had to say. Was she getting remarried? She hadn't ever mentioned that she was dating, but then, he supposed that would be awkward.

"I miss Daisy," she said plainly, and Nick felt his heart skip a beat.

Was she here to discuss custody? He'd gotten comfortable with the arrangement, and even though he knew that Daisy missed her mother and he wished that things could be different, the thought of not spending every day with his daughter wasn't an option for him.

"She misses you too," he said tightly.

Knowing that Daisy was just upstairs and probably not asleep yet, he motioned to the patio doors. "It's a nice night. Let's sit outside."

Once they were out of earshot and settled on the wicker conversation set that his parents had given him as a housewarming gift, he took a few gulps of the cool evening air, but it did nothing to settle the anxiety that was building in his chest. He set his wineglass on the nearest end table. He needed a clear head tonight.

Liz sipped her wine, looking out over the yard where some of Daisy's toys were scattered.

"It's nice here," she said. "Peaceful."

He nodded. "I'm happy here. Daisy is too." The words were a warning. Maybe a plea. If he had to move to Seattle to be with his daughter, he would, but that's not what he wanted. And he didn't think Daisy did either.

She smiled at him. "I can see that. You're more relaxed here. More...fulfilled. Daisy seems happier than she was when we lived in Boston. It makes me a little sad, actually."

He looked at her in surprise. "How so?"

She shrugged and looked out into the distance, where two squirrels were chasing each other on tree branches.

"I feel bad about how things were between us those last few months," she said. When she looked at him, her eyes were filled with tears. "We hadn't been happy in so long that it was easier to think about starting over than trying to make it work. I was so focused on everything I had given up that I didn't stop to think that one day I might regret giving up on us."

The yard felt suddenly very quiet, only the sounds of nature filling the air.

"I want to try again," she said, reaching out to take his hand. "I want to be a family. For Daisy. For me. For all of us."

His heart was pounding now, and even though he was looking into Liz's eyes, his mind was on Daisy, as it always was. Daisy would be overjoyed to have her mother in her life every day and to be a family of three again. To have both of her parents under the same roof.

But like Liz had said—and so many others—Daisy was happy.

And he couldn't ruin that for her.

"This is a lot to think about," he said gruffly.

"Just think about it. My job allows me to work remotely.

I'd still travel, but this could be my home base." She squeezed his hand a little tighter. "This could be my home. Our home, Nick. All of us."

He pulled in a breath and nodded. He wasn't ready to make a decision. Not yet. Not when there wasn't an easy solution.

Years ago, when he'd found out he was going to be a father, it was more clear what he had to do. But now there was history, and baggage, and he couldn't forget the fights and arguments, that empty feeling that came and went as quickly as the reminder that all he needed was Daisy.

She was his purpose. He had to do what was best for her.

Even if he didn't know if that was what was best for both of them.

Carly was up before her alarm the next morning and the house was still dark when she tiptoed downstairs after a quick shower. As much as she craved a cup of strong coffee to get her going, she didn't want to wake Nana, and not only because she wanted to let her sleep.

She hadn't seen her grandmother or her sisters yesterday at the carnival, only she probably had herself to blame for that. After Nick's ex-wife showed up, she'd power walked to the car and come back here where she tried again to work on her article and eventually gave up, going to bed early even though she wasn't tired.

Now, she tried to push the image of the woman from her mind as she let herself out the front door and walked into town, guided by the light of the moon that shined high above. There was a sweet smell of flowers and freshly cut grass that made her smile, but it did little to keep the unsettling feeling at bay.

Yesterday at least one thing in her life had felt promising, but now everything—including Nick—felt more uncertain than ever.

Carly walked around to the back of the bakery and saw both of her sisters' cars parked side by side. All thoughts of Nick momentarily gone, she took a deep breath and pushed through the door, giving a tentative smile to Becca when she traded her handbag for the apron.

The coffeepot was brewing and she stared at it longingly, waiting for it to finish.

"You're here earlier than usual," Jill said from the counter where she was icing a fresh tray of cinnamon rolls.

So she was still speaking to her. That was a good sign.

"Couldn't sleep," she admitted, reaching for one of the mugs bearing their store logo. She realized with a pang that she didn't have one back at her apartment in Philadelphia. That when she'd left, she'd been so determined to start her life fresh that she chose to leave all the parts of Hope Hollow behind her.

Even the good ones.

"Too excited about your contest entry?" Jill asked.

Carly poured herself a mug of coffee and turned to her sister, seeing a set jaw instead of a smile.

"So you are mad," she observed.

"Not mad," Becca interjected. "Just...surprised. Why didn't you tell us you were entering?"

"Well, for starters, Nana is a judge, and even though it's blind judging, if she'd known I was entering, she would have probably been off the panel. And she was really looking forward to it."

Becca nodded, but Jill just slapped bread dough onto the counter and began kneading it a little harder than necessary.

"She probably wouldn't have known with that recipe. It doesn't look like anything you've made before." Jill stopped working to raise an eyebrow.

"Actually, it's a favorite recipe around my office. The decorations were new, though. Daisy inspired me. She loves unicorns and so do all of her friends."

"So this is what kept you from helping out at the bakery these past few days?" Jill shook her head. "You talked about wanting to help out but you went off and did your own thing in the end once again."

"That's not what I did!" Carly set her mug down. She stared at her sister, seeing the anger and hurt in her eyes. "That's not what I ever intended, then or now, Jill. When I left for college, it just became easier to stay away. And it's not like either of you ever called and asked me to come back."

"And would you have even come?" Jill said archly.

"Maybe," Carly said. "Probably. If I knew you needed me."

Jill's expression softened before she picked up the dough and slammed it back on the counter. "Forget it. It doesn't matter."

"I did it for the bakery, Jill!" Carly said, staring at Becca for assistance, but unlike usual, her middle sister was frowning, standing firmly at Jill's side.

It was just like the old days when the two of them would boss her around, always on the same page, always seeing her as the kid sister, the tagalong, the one who wasn't part of the decision-making process.

"This bakery prides itself on family recipes," Jill said firmly.

"And I'm family!" Carly cried. She realized that her eyes were burning, hot with tears that she was fighting back, emotions that she had kept at bay. At a safe distance.

But now she was here, facing the hard conversation because there was no other time to have it. Because she couldn't just start fresh now. Not when she already knew what her life was like in Philly.

And what her life could have been like here. Or still could be.

"This is about Nick, isn't it?" Jill asked.

Carly felt her cheeks pale. "No. Why do you say that?"

Had she seen them yesterday, before Daisy's mother walked in? Did her sisters know she was in town? People talked around here; it was bound to get out, especially around the carnival, where everyone was gathered.

"Because you two have been spending a lot of time together teaming up with ideas for this place. Is that it? You think if you turn the bakery around, you'll have a second chance with Nick?" Jill was waiting for an answer.

Carly realized with a strange sensation that this was exactly what she'd been hoping, just not in the way that Jill thought.

Somewhere in the last two weeks, she went from thinking that saving this bakery was the answer to her getting that promotion at the magazine to a reason for staying in town.

And maybe, getting back together with Nick.

Only now Nick's ex-wife was in town. And the bakery was no better off than it had been this time last week.

Slowly, she untied the strings at her waist and looped her apron over the hook near the framed photo of the Sunrise Sisters, the three women who were raised in this very kitchen, meant to carry on the recipes like the one in the very bowl that Carly was holding in the picture.

She felt a pain deep in her heart. One of fresh loss, nearly as deep as the one she'd experienced the first time she walked in here, knowing her mother never would again.

She'd been crazy to think that she could hold on to her past when she'd fought so hard to let it go.

Liz slept in Daisy's room, in the spare bed usually reserved for slumber parties. When she came downstairs, Nick suggested they go to the park, where Daisy could play and they could talk.

He'd always been a firm believer that everything was clearer in the mornings, and today he hoped that he was right. His future was riding on it.

So was Daisy's welfare.

They walked to the park near the end of Main Street where Daisy immediately ran to the swings.

Liz brushed her hand against his and then reached for it. Nick felt his back stiffen and he knew that it was time to be honest with both Liz and himself.

"I've thought a lot about what you said last night," he said, stuffing his hands into his pockets. "You were right about a lot of things. Daisy is happy here. And back in Boston, I wasn't happy and neither were you."

And maybe, neither was Daisy.

He paused, knowing what he had to say. Hoping that Daisy would find it in her heart to understand someday.

"You and me, we're getting along better than we have in years."

"I know!" Liz exclaimed.

He shook his head, holding up a hand. "But I think that's because we've taken some space. We're both living the life that makes us happy as individuals. Separately."

She frowned at him. "What are you saying?"

"I'm saying that I think if we got back together it would only be a matter of time before things went back to the way they were. We were forcing something that wasn't there. You said that a hundred times, and I'm saying it now. I didn't want to believe it before, but you were right. We tried our best, Liz, and it wasn't enough."

"But what about Daisy? Aren't you thinking of what's best for her?"

"That's all I ever think about," he ground out. "And that's the other thing you were right about. Daisy is happy. She's thriving. And she's getting older. And I just don't think that seeing her parents arguing and unhappy all the time is what's best for her. I think she'll be happiest if we're happy too."

Liz lifted her eyebrows, but she didn't reply. Instead, she shook her head and then dropped onto a bench. "Maybe you're right," she finally said.

Nick sat down beside her. This time, he was the one to

reach for her hand. "We both want the same thing. The same thing we always wanted. For Daisy to be happy. That's what brought us together in the first place. That's what kept us together even though we were never really in love with each other. Even though you always wondered what life might have been if you had the chance to find that guy you were head over heels for—"

"Nick." A tear slipped down her cheek. "I'm sorry."

He gave her a small smile. "We both tried our best. There's nothing for either of us to apologize for. We have a beautiful daughter together, and that's something you and I are going to share for the rest of our lives. And I'm grateful for that. And for all the memories we made together."

"If I had to do it all over again, I would," Liz said sadly.

Nick pulled in a breath, knowing that was only half true for him. He'd never take back a second he spent with Daisy.

But there was room for someone else in his heart, too. And this time, he wasn't going to let her go if he could help it.

Carly decided to cut through the park, eager to get home before anyone on Main Street could pop their heads out of their shop doors and ask her about the contest entry. She kept her head low and her pace brisk, not even slowing to admire the first tulips to have sprung, but when she got to the edge of the park, she ground to a halt. Her heart felt like it could beat right out of her body. There was Nick, on a bench, holding another woman's hand. And not just any woman's hand. His ex-wife's hand. Daisy's mother's hand.

They looked so natural together. So fitting. So right. Like two people who could talk easily, who shared more than she could ever have known or experienced. Good times. Bad times. Holidays. Years of life together. A child.

Maybe, from the looks of it, a future.

She turned quickly, before one of them spotted her—or worse—Daisy would wave and smile and call her over.

Just thinking that she might never see that little girl again pulled at her heart almost as much as the thought of not seeing Nick again.

But that's what it had come to, wasn't it? That's the way it had always been. The plan was to never see Nick again.

Just like the plan had been to come to town, write her article, and go back to Philadelphia for her promotion.

She looked back before she crossed the street, this time to see Nick reach over and pull the woman in for a long hug.

And for the second time in her life, there was nothing Carly could do but accept that she had no place in his life.

The house was quiet when Carly returned, and she assumed no one was home until she walked into the kitchen and saw her grandmother in the backyard. She had a watering pail in her hand, but she wasn't focused on any of the flowers that were blooming daily now.

Nana was standing on her tiptoes, like a teenage girl if

Carly closed her eyes and blocked out the grey hair—and she was staring intently through that hole in the hedge.

Carly watched with widening eyes as Nana leaned in closer and then, clearly satisfied, backed away, looking anything but pleased as she came into the house.

"See anything interesting?" Carly asked in a knowing tone.

Nana looked flustered as she kicked off her gardening clogs. "Just making sure my arborvitae are staying hydrated. One bad winter and that's all it takes to ruin them."

Carly made a show of looking out the window over the sink. "Oh, they look hardy to me. I'd have thought that big hole would be what caused them distress."

"It's not a *big* hole." Nana tsked and went to fill the kettle.

"No, then it would be too noticeable, I suppose." Carly caught her grandmother's eye and lost her grip on her smile, letting it slip through. "What's really going on, Nana? Is this about Frannie? Is she trying to beat you in some gardening club event? Or—" She couldn't believe she hadn't thought of it before.

"This is about Mr. Quincy, isn't it?" she asked.

"What?" Nana frowned and dropped the kettle back on the stovetop. "What are you talking about? He lives on the opposite side of my house."

"Yes, but I bet if I went and looked through that hole in the hedge, I'd see that he was next door at Frannie's at the very moment."

"And who cares if he is?" Nana asked, avoiding eye contact.

"I think you care, Nana," Carly said gently. "Is it so wrong to like the man back?"

"Yes," Nana said forcefully, surprising her. "It is wrong."

"Because of Becca? Because he's Jonah's grandfather?" Carly knew that neither of her sisters held the poor man responsible for his grandson's behavior.

"That's just one more reason," Nana said with a nod. "Thanks for reminding me."

Carly blinked at her grandmother, surprised by the emotion in her voice. "But why is it so wrong? He's sweet. He's your neighbor. He loves dogs. And if I didn't know better, I'd say he loves you too."

"Or Frannie." Nana sniffed.

"Ever think he's just trying to make you jealous?" Carly asked. "I've seen the way he looks at you. Nothing has changed in all these years."

"You're right," Nana replied. "It hasn't. And it won't."

"What's that supposed to mean?" Carly asked.

"It means that I still love your grandfather. He was my soulmate. The love of my life. He's irreplaceable." Suddenly, Nana's eyes filled with tears and she shook her head, turning her back to face the stove.

Carly felt her shoulders droop when she stared at the back of her grandmother's head, knowing that her grandmother always kept a stiff upper lip. She wouldn't want Carly to see her like this. Hurting. Down.

Not then. Not now.

"You're right," Carly said softly as she set a hand on her grandmother's shoulder. "Nothing has changed in all these years. Some things don't have to. But maybe, there's room for both."

Nana shook her head, but after a moment she reached up and patted Carly's hand. "I'm not sure I know how to do that."

She turned and looked at Carly now. "I guess I'm afraid of what will happen if I let go."

"But you've held on so tight, Nana. I'm at fault for that too. It's...why I stayed away for so long. It was easier that way. I thought I was moving on but all I was really doing was holding on to the past. Letting it decide my present. And my future."

"I know, my girl," Nana said softly.

"Is that why you never pressured me to come back?" Carly asked.

"I knew you would when you were ready. You just had to find your way." She gave a little grin. "But you still kept the best parts about yourself true. You kept baking."

Carly pulled in a breath. They hadn't talked about the contest entry, and now there was no denying it.

"I couldn't tell you since you were judging," she said. "But...I didn't think I'd win." Hoped she would win, sure, but as she'd learned so many times, hope was far different than reality.

"Of course you'd win! You're a Parker! Baking is in your blood." Nana beamed with pride. "My granddaughter, the winner!"

"So, you're not mad?" Carly worried.

"Mad? Honey, you made something beautiful and delicious. And you beat the pants of Frannie James and her pie," she said with a mischievous gleam in her eye. "I couldn't be more proud. And no one can say the contest was rigged since I had absolutely no idea! You were clever not to tell me," Nana added with a wink.

Carly felt her shoulders sink. "That's not the only reason I didn't tell you," she said. "I worried that you'd think I was... overstepping, by making one of my own recipes."

Nana frowned at her. "But all I ever wanted you girls to do was love baking as much as your mother and I did. And my mother before me."

"But all the traditions at Sunrise. About keeping it in the family. Making the family recipes."

Nana nodded thoughtfully and turned off the stove when the kettle started to steam. "It's true, but somewhere along the way, I guess I stopped thinking that there could be room for new recipes in our family."

Carly gave her a small smile. "There could be room for a lot of good things, Nana."

Nana looked at her for a long moment and then reached out to squeeze her hands. "You came back to town just in time, Carly."

Carly wanted to believe that, but she wasn't so sure.

If anything, she'd come back too late.

Seventeen

This was it. Sunday. The day she was supposed to be packing up her things, loading up the trunk, and driving back to Philadelphia, her home of ten years.

But it wasn't home at all. And when Carly woke to the sun peeking through the curtains and the smell of Nana's famous cinnamon rolls baking in the kitchen, she knew that despite its hardships, setbacks, and disappointments, Hope Hollow was where her heart was.

It was with Nick. And Daisy. Even if they had someone else.

It was the bakery, even though the beloved sign would soon be replaced with a corporate logo.

It was in the recipes that her sisters made each day, the ones that had been taught to them by their mother and grandmother.

It was in this house, where the best and worst moments of her life had been lived.

And shared.

In Philadelphia, her world was safe, but it was empty. And here, it was full.

She tossed on jeans and a sweater and braided her long hair. Downstairs, the coffee pulled her to the kitchen, and she smiled to see Nana bending down to remove the tray of cinnamon rolls from the oven.

"Those smell heavenly," Carly sighed, her mouth watering.

"Too bad they aren't for you," Nana said.

Carly frowned at her, but then she noticed that her grandmother was already dressed for the day and—more than that—she was wearing lipstick. At—Carly glanced at the clock—nine in the morning!

"I really slept in," she muttered aloud. Then, looking a little closer at her grandmother, she said, "Social plans?"

"Something like that," Nana's voice turned coy.

Now, Carly couldn't help but smile. "You mean...a certain neighbor?"

"Robert always came in on Sundays for the cinnamon rolls," Nana replied, her cheeks turning pink as she transferred the rolls to a large plate and then smothered them in icing.

Ah, so Mr. Quincy was Robert now?

"More like he came in to see you and the cinnamon rolls were his excuse," Carly replied, and Nana's pinched mouth turned into a shy smile.

She heaved a sigh as she picked up the plate, her eyes bright when they met Carly. "I can't believe I'm really doing this."

"I can. And I'm happy for you, Nana." Carly hesitated.

"Can I ask what made you change your mind?"

Nana looked thoughtful for a moment. "I guess it was you winning the baking contest."

"Me?" Carly was astonished. "And here I thought you'd say that you weren't about to let Fannie steal your man."

Nana laughed. "Well, maybe that too. But...I never allowed myself to move on. I guess I was afraid of change. But seeing how you took something from your past and grew it into something new, made me realize that you'd done exactly what I'd always wanted you to do. You followed your heart. But more than that, you were *true* to your heart. And I knew it was okay for me to do the same."

Carly wanted nothing more at that moment than to pull her grandmother in for a long, much-needed embrace, but she also knew that warm cinnamon rolls were the best, and that poor Robert Quincy had waited long enough.

"Wish me luck," Nana said, moving toward the hallway.

"Oh, you won't need it," Carly assured her as she opened the front door for her grandmother. "I think Mr. Quincy is in for the surprise of his life."

"That makes two of you," Nana said. She gave Carly a glance over her shoulder as she walked down the pathway toward the sidewalk. "Jill called this morning. I think you'll want to hear what she has to say."

Carly closed the door slowly, and even though she'd had every intention of watching her grandmother out the window the way Nana most certainly would have done had the situation been reversed, her curiosity was too great.

Jill wanted to talk to her. And from the sound of her grandmother's voice, Carly had reason to hope that it might just be good news.

Sunday mornings in the bakery were usually the busiest time of the week, and Carly was pleased to see that today was no exception. She entered through the front door, noticing that every table was filled—and that everyone seemed happy with the new arrangement.

Even Jill from the looks of it.

Carly felt her shoulders relax when Jill looked up from the bakery case and waved her over, her smile bigger than Carly had seen it since she'd been back in town.

She moved her way around the line of families and met her sister at the end of the counter near the kitchen door, leaving Becca to handle the crowd.

"Look at all these people!" Carly exclaimed, but then, seeing Becca push a strand of loose hair from her forehead in a flustered motion, she winced. "I should have come in early. To help."

"I'm just glad that I caught you before you left town," Jill said. She looked pained when she reached for Carly's wrist. "I'm sorry, Carly. I've been unfair. Not just in our argument but...maybe always."

"Not always," Carly said ruefully. "And I get it. You've been here running the bakery, always doing what you thought was best. I overstepped."

"More like saved the place," Jill said with a snort. "All these people? They're asking about your cupcakes! And some others have asked about cookies shaped like unicorns?"

Carly laughed, delighted. "Daisy's cookies! But wait... All these people are here for my sweets?"

Jill nodded. "That's right. And if I thought I was in trouble two weeks ago, I'll be in more trouble if I don't fill these orders."

Carly looked at her. "Does that mean...?" She was almost afraid to say it, to feel the last breath of hope be snuffed out.

But Jill just grinned. "I'm not selling if that's what you're asking. How could I now when we have all this new demand?"

Carly laughed and hugged her sister. A long, proper hug that she needed more than she knew.

"I just wish that I didn't have to leave," she said, knowing that there was no way around it.

"You can give us the recipes," Jill said hopefully. "I promise to do right by them."

"I wouldn't doubt it for a second," Carly said. She took in the line of people, the flurry of energy as Becca nodded and scribbled on a notepad, and then, when she turned back to Jill, the gleam of pure happiness in her sister's eyes.

"You did it, Carly," Jill said.

"No, *we* did it. I couldn't have done it without you. Or Mom. Or Nana. They taught us to bake. And they taught us to love this place." Carly swallowed against the lump in her throat. "And you always loved it most of all. You just have a stubborn way of showing it."

Jill looked down. "I just wanted to keep everything the way it was...when Mom was still here."

Carly felt her eyes burn with tears as she reached out to squeeze her sister's hand. The same hand that she used to hold when crossing the street, sometimes against her will, only at Jill's insistence.

She smiled now, thinking of how responsible her sister had always been. How much she cared.

"Everything you've done for this place comes from the best intentions," Carly said. "And the only thing that Mom and Nana ever taught us was that everything we baked, everything we did, should be done with love."

Jill blinked away her own tears when she met Carly's eyes, and for a quiet moment, they shared a smile of understanding that sometimes only distance could provide.

"I know you were upset when I stayed away after college."

"Carly—" Jill shook her head but Carly had to say it. It was long overdue.

"I thought I'd be happier, doing my own thing, not bogged down by the past. But the past is always going to be a part of me. And those cupcakes are proof of that. Everything that matters is here, in this bakery. In this town."

Now Jill looked at her cautiously. "Does that mean... But you have an apartment. A job."

"An apartment that I need to pack. And I job that I need to leave," Carly said. She pulled in a breath, feeling lighter than she had in longer than she could remember. "That is...if you're hiring."

"Hiring?" Jill cried. "Honey, you're family. This bakery was always your home. I'm just sorry if you didn't feel like it was." Then, lowering her voice, she said, "This doesn't have anything to do with Nick, does it?"

Carly felt her smile droop nearly as much as her heart. "No," she said sadly. "I gave up hope on Nick a long time ago."

"I think we both lost our hope recently," Jill said, a little smile creeping up. "But the Sunrise Sisters always manage to see the bright side." She gave a little nudge with her chin. "Turn around."

Carly frowned at her sister, not knowing what she was getting at, but like she always did, she obeyed her eldest sister and turned.

And there, standing in the doorway, smiling at her, was Nick.

~

"Nick." Carly's heart was thumping as she approached him. She scanned the tables around him, looking for Daisy, possibly Daisy's mother, thinking of a dozen reasons why he would be here right now. This was a bakery, after all, and it was a Sunday morning.

But the softness in his gaze told her that he wasn't here for the cinnamon rolls or even to place an order for her cupcakes.

"I was afraid I was too late," he said.

Her chest lifted. Ten years ago, she might have said that

he was, that he'd hurt her too badly, that they'd missed their chance.

But she'd had time to move on. Or at least move away. And after all these years, he was still the one for her.

And now, she dared to think that she was the one for him, too.

Just as quickly, she remembered what she'd seen yesterday. The park. The bench. The way he reached out and held his ex-wife's hand and didn't let go. The way they'd held each other, probably long after Carly had walked away.

"Just barely," she said, watching the smile slip from his eyes. "I'm supposed to be heading out soon. I just...needed to come here first."

Nick nodded slowly and then gestured to the door. "I guess I'll walk you out then?"

Carly hitched her handbag higher on her shoulder and walked out into the warm sunshine. "Daisy's not with you?"

He shook his head, looking regretful, like there was something he couldn't say.

"She's with her mother," Carly said with a small smile. "It's okay, Nick. I understand. That's her mother. The three of you...you're a family."

"We were a family," Nick corrected.

"But..." Carly looked up at him, deciding that there was no reason to hold back now. "I saw you. Yesterday, on my way home. At the park."

Nick looked confused for a minute and then said, "What you saw was two people with a long history. Two people that recognized that they are better off apart. It was a conversation that was long overdue and one that needed to happen for both of us to fully move on."

Her heart was hammering now. She looked up at him, still not certain of what he was saying, but daring to hope that it was what she longed to hear.

"Move on?"

He gave a quick nod and then said, "I know I'm too late. I know you're going back to Philadelphia today. I know that I have no right to ask you to stay. But you asked me the other day if there's anything I would have done differently and I realized that there was. I'd never take back all the moments I shared with Daisy, but forcing a relationship with Liz wasn't fair to either one of us. Or you. You were always there, Carly, like an unfinished story. And I always wondered what might have been."

She stared up at him, pushing back the tears that threatened to fall. Her voice was thick when she said, "Now you don't have to wonder. Now you know."

He nodded softly. "I know. It's good to see you happy, Carly. It's good to know that you've...moved on."

"Moved away," she corrected. "But my heart was always here. In this town. In this bakery." She motioned to the shop, thinking of her sisters inside, the newfound excitement they had, the celebration they would all have when she returned in two long weeks.

"I'm leaving today to give my notice at work," she told Nick. "That article was meant to lead to my future. And it did. Because it took me back to my past."

"You mean you're moving back for good?"

"My sisters are going to need my help running the bakery

now that business is booming again. Besides, do you really think I could leave without saying goodbye to Daisy?" she said as he slid his arms around her waist.

"So I finally get to know how things might have been," he said. "We finally get to know how our ending turns out."

"Happily," she told him, as he leaned down to kiss her.

epilogue

Sunrise Bakery closed—but only for two weeks. Renovations were needed, and taste-testing too. Daisy was, of course, all too happy to volunteer.

The old striped awning was replaced with a scalloped edge sign in their signature shade of yellow, but that wasn't the only thing about it that had been modified.

Carly was surprised that Nana had suggested the change—but more so that Jill agreed to go along with it. Jill, however, was surprisingly open to new ideas these days, and once they all started brainstorming, the excitement grew between them all. The tables were painted white and the chairs a buttery yellow. The menu that hung over the counter now boasted their newest items, and several old favorites as well. There would always be cinnamon rolls on the weekends, and the Mother's Day pie, of course. There would still be the holiday bread, and there was no way they'd ever consider taking the strawberry pie off the menu.

Or their mother's favorite chocolate chip cookies, now renamed in her honor.

Or Daisy's oatmeal cookies.

Opening day came all too soon, and Carly felt almost as nervous as Jill looked when they gathered in the kitchen, tired from a long morning spent baking.

"They're going to love it," Becca assured them, but even she looked a little uncertain. "I know we've been over everything and baking since before dawn, but I can't help but feel like there's something missing."

Carly had that feeling too, and she couldn't figure out what it was until they all took a moment to look around the kitchen, which had also received a facelift thanks to Nana's investment. The new ovens gleamed, and the canisters of sugar and chocolate chips and colorful sprinkles brightened the room. But the counter that had remained untouched felt empty.

Carly walked into the small office and pulled out Nana's recipe book, which she carried back into the kitchen and set on the counter.

"This needs a proper home," she said, dusting off the cover. "I think it deserves to be displayed out front, where everyone can see it."

"Just so long as no one tries stealing any of my recipes," Nana joked. They all knew, of course, that she'd be flattered if they did. The recipes were meant to be shared. And enjoyed.

But something was still missing. Carly's hands shook a little as she walked over to the wall and removed the framed photo. She carried it back to the counter and then flipped to the back of the recipe book, her heart warming when her eyes met her mother's, and for that one, perfect moment, it was like she was right here again.

Where a part of her would always be.

Silently, she removed the backing of the frame and slipped the photograph over the other.

"There," she said, holding it up for everyone. "This is what was missing."

Nana gave a little gasp as she walked over to take the frame. "I've been looking for this photograph for years. I thought I lost it."

"You did," Carly told her, wiping away a tear. They'd all lost a little something in these four walls.

But they'd all found something too.

"Let's go outside together and welcome our customers," Becca said, holding out both of her hands.

"You girls go on ahead," Nana told them, giving them a warm smile of encouragement. "This is your day to enjoy."

She held the frame tight in her hands, and Carly knew that she needed a moment to herself, in the kitchen where so many wonderful memories had been made.

Jill and Carly each took hold of Becca, firmly in the middle, as she quietly led them through the storefront, past the counter that was filled with the evidence of an early morning's work, only stopping at the glass-paned front door.

It was a beautiful spring day. Blue skies, no clouds, and flowers blooming in the new window boxes.

Becca paused, waited for Jill to give her nod of approval, and then turned the sign on the door. Jill undid the locks, and Carly reached for the big easel they all helped to carry outside, alerting everyone that they were open.

Soon, Carly knew, old and new customers would come inside, some out of curiosity, some out of habit. But for now, they all stood back and took in the look of the place, their gazes all resting on the new, but not improved, logo.

Nana's idea. To many, including them, this would always be the Sunrise Bakery.

But today, it officially became the Sunrise Sisters Bakery.

about the author

Olivia Miles is a *USA Today* bestselling author of women's fiction and contemporary romance. She has frequently been ranked as an Amazon Top 100 author, and her books have appeared on several bestseller lists, including Amazon charts, Barnes and Noble, BookScan, and *USA Today*. Olivia lives on the North Shore of Chicago with her family and an adorable pair of dogs.

Visit www.OliviaMilesBooks.com for more.